BOMB TWO

BOMB TWO

A Novel

Major Don Henderson

BUCHAN & ENRIGHT, PUBLISHERS
LONDON

To my late wife Joan, for her
love and support

First published in 1983 by
Buchan & Enright, Publishers, Limited
53 Fleet Street, London EC4Y 1BE

ISBN 0 907675 13 1

Printed and bound in Great Britain by
Richard Clay (The Chaucer Press) Ltd
Bungay, Suffolk

One

The cold, dank, swirling fog was riven by an intense glow of yellow-orange light, followed instantly by a muted roar of killer noise and then a rapidly dwindling rumble of competing echoes, bouncing off nearby buildings.

In the fleeting, total silence which followed, the world seemed to hold its breath, until released from the spell by the thud of falling fragments and the tinkling sound of broken glass. The Metropolitan Police inspector moved half a pace farther back into the shelter of the police lodge porch, crouching very slightly and turning his head away from the sound. It was 6.40 a.m.

'The bloody thing's gone up!' he said to the constable at his side. 'What's happened to our man? Can't see a damned thing in this fog! Still, I'm not waiting to find out. Get on the trumpet for an ambulance and then to the nick. Tell them that there's been an explosion and the Explosives Officer may have been injured. Quick as you can!'

Arriving at Greenwich police station at 5.35 a.m. that morning, early for his shift—a habit grafted on to most policemen who used to have to parade fifteen minutes before off, in their own time—he had parked his car and looked in at the station office to let them know that he was about. Pausing to have a quick word with a colleague, he overheard the station officer, a sergeant, accepting a call from the Information Room at Scotland Yard.

'There's a message about a bomb in the Royal Naval College. No location given but it's due to explode before seven. Coded and the usual Irish male anon. Timed at 05.39.'

Because the call had come in so close to the end of the night shift he volunteered to take it, and went off to find his driver, like himself an early bird.

Arriving at the college gates he was taken in to the Ministry of Defence Police duty officer and quickly explained why he was there. A quick discussion between them settled on the Painted Hall as being the most likely area—a prestige target with considerable propaganda potential.

Moving off down the road through the darkness, their feet crunching on the frosty road surface, the two duty officers stayed silent, each enveloped in his own thoughts, their torches doing little to penetrate the fog. On reaching the foot of the steps leading up to the Painted Hall, the 'Met' inspector explained briefly that it would be wise if only one at a time was at risk and that they should leap-frog forward from whatever cover was available, and then climbed the steps, directing his torch from side to side.

Putting his left foot on the half-way step, he could dimly discern a pair of large doors ahead of him and, playing the less than brilliant beam over them, could hardly believe his eyes. The circle of light framed a plain, dark duffle bag, hanging on one of the doorknobs. His stomach lurched and he held his breath, then turned and hurried down the steps. He had not been prepared for this—he hadn't really taken the threat seriously and had been more or less going through the motions. There'd been quite a few nuisance calls recently, but, of course, they had all to be checked out.

The two men retraced their steps to the lodge, and passed the news of a confirmed object. They would need an explosives officer. Time: 05.55.

In the fog-reinforced darkness, there was no chance of getting a look at the scene of the explosion from where he was standing. Not having a radio link with the Explosives Officer didn't help either. All right, there would be good operational reasons against such a link but it still didn't help.

'OK. So go up and look for yourself,' the inspector told himself. But what about a second one? Admittedly he had seen only one object when he had gone up before, but he hadn't waited around to check, had he? And, if there *had* been two, which one had gone off? If two, were they both on timers?

The Explosives Officer's driver materialised at the porch like a wraith out of the fog. He had been sitting in the Range Rover, positioned in the yard opposite, and manning the radios, ready to respond to any demand from Joe Hawke.

'I don't like it, guv,' he said. 'I've had no call from Joe and I'm sure that he would have let me know if he's OK. As far as I could make out, the explosion was at the King's Entrance and that's just where he would be.'

The inspector did not hesitate. 'Right, I'll go and see what the score is. Have you got a better light than this thing of mine? It's dimmer than the proverbial Toc H lamp.' He turned to his own driver. 'Wait here for the ambulance. It should be on its way by now. I'll come up on the PR when I've found out what's happening.'

Cautiously inching his way towards the stone steps, he risked a quick flash from the hand lamp. Once again that sickening jolt. Where the beautiful doors had been was now a gaping hole, outlined by splintered stone. Moving forward, he could see shattered stonework and other fragments lying in the area.

Then, above the scrunching sound of his careful advance, he heard a sound that brought him to an immediate halt in mid-stride. A deep groan and the faintest rustle of movement came out of the clammy darkness off to the left of the doors.

Unclipping his PR handset he told his driver to send the ambulance down as soon as it arrived, then moved quickly up the steps, pausing fractionally at the top and directing the lamp beam to the left. Bringing it to a halt at the foot of the stone balustrade, he felt his bile rising, the cold knifing through his clothing and into his very core.

Disregarding all else—the rescue of the injured took total precedence—he dashed forward to kneel down beside the recumbent, twisted figure of Joe Hawke, jammed against the stonework. Clad in a damaged flak jacket and wearing a heavily scarred helmet with its visor ripped off, he was lying in a steadily growing pool of blood, breathing stertorously, a slight froth of blood at the corner of his mouth. His right arm was lying at an unnatural angle, a gaping rent above the right knee of his trousers revealed a deep wound in the thigh, and white bone showed through a jagged split under his right eye.

Faintly, through the fog, the inspector could hear the familiar two-tone sound announcing an ambulance's approach. He took out a clean handkerchief and folded it into a pad, and as he pressed it over the wound in Joe's leg, was relieved to see that the blood was seeping out quite steadily and not pulsing in the bright red gouts that would signal damage to an artery. As the handkerchief was pressed on his leg, the crumpled figure stirred and uttered another deep groan.

'Don't worry, Joe. I can hear the ambulance coming and they'll look after you. Just lie still.'

Joe Hawke relapsed into unconsciousness as the ambulance, its klaxon now silenced, pulled up at the bottom of the steps. The inspector played the lamp's beam on the top step and called out to the crew, directing their approach. In less than a minute they joined him at Hawke's side, and with a few deft movements, manoeuvred the casualty on to the metal-framed stretcher that they had brought with them.

Two-tone again demanding priority, the ambulance sped out of the College gates while the inspector made his way back to the Range Rover where he gave the driver the expected bad news. To the background of fog-horns grunting their doleful message, he headed for the warmth of the police lodge, and the telephone. His feeling of weary desolation was deepened by the realisation that he was now faced with composing a lengthy pocketbook entry—to be followed by other shots in the interminable paper war when he got back to the nick. Could there possibly be a correlation between the increase in quantity and complexity of the paperwork and the falling clear-up rate?

It came to him that he had forgotten to ask the driver—now well on his way to the hospital—which Explosives Officer would be coming down to the scene to finish off. They were sure to send another one and he would have to be here when they arrived.

The blue Ford Cortina III being driven along Crawford Street in London's West End was unremarkable—a nondescript, volume-production family saloon in average condition, except for a piece of chrome trim missing from the nearside rear door, being driven in a wholly law-abiding manner. All three occupants were young and fit, all were fanatical supporters and members of the Irish National Liberation Army, but that was just about all that they had in common. They were just finishing a busy night—a successful one by their standards.

Just after six o'clock that morning, Ryan Kelly and Michael O'Byrne had made their stealthy way into the heart of the Royal Naval College where, at 5.25 a.m., Kelly had placed and armed the bag bomb. In his role as 'placer', his revolver had remained in his raincoat pocket but O'Byrne was the 'minder', the traditional Irish gunman. His function was to position himself behind a solid pillar at the corner of the balustrade with his Uzi machine-carbine drawn and cocked, covering all the approaches against interference. The gut-wrenching, sweaty tension had increased perceptibly once the bomb was running and they had lost no time in moving away from its danger area into the shelter of King Charles Block; Ryan's revolver was now drawn, so that they were now giving each other mutual protection.

Making their way through the swirling fog to the very edge of the river, they had gained the River Walk, then crept quietly away to the river end of King William Walk and, skirting the beached and silent *Cutty Sark* with its modern companion, Sir Francis Chichester's *Gypsy Moth IV*, reached the top of the circular staircase. Time: 05.35.

At about this time Liam Hughes, the third member of their Active Service Unit, was telephoning the bomb call to Scotland Yard from a phone box in Poplar on the other side of the river. This procedure, common in Belfast, relied upon everybody sticking to planned timings, and had produced, in Ulster, a number of unexpected, occasionally macabre, situations, but was calculated to hinder subsequent investigation by the police.

This done, he drove the Ford Cortina, stolen two days earlier in Willesden, towards the Isle of Dogs rendezvous.

From the bottom of the staircase, the two bombers set off northwards along the cold, damp tunnel stretching away under the river to its termination, a quarter of a mile away, under the Isle of Dogs. Unlike the other three public tunnels, this one provided no facilities for vehicular traffic and was used solely by pedestrians.

Some fifteen minutes later they emerged in Island Gardens, to be enveloped once more in the penetrating, frost-laden blanket spreading outwards from the river, and set off warily in the direction of the rendezvous. They would have been wise to check the garden, for their return to ground level had been observed by the beady eyes of a piece of human flotsam sheltering nearby. The tramp had spent many years merging silently into the shadows under the protection of an intruder-warning system which could stand comparison with radar. The event would later become known to the police.

Turning the corner into Macquarie Way they could just discern a parked car and, moving cautiously towards it, were relieved to find that Hughes was sitting, silent and unmoving, in the driver's seat. Recognising them, he leaned across to release the button on the rear door and they climbed in to sink thankfully into the rear seat.

Liam Hughes was not, strictly, an Irishman, having been born and brought up in Cardiff. In the mid-nineteenth century, the railways had introduced into South Wales cheap labour in the form of Irish navvies, a proportion of whom settled there, eventually to be assimilated. There were some, however, who still persisted in a distorted loyalty to their country of origin, and he was one such. Aged twenty-four, short, muscular, with black hair and a permanently blue chin, Hughes' mixed Irish-Welsh parentage had endowed him with a restless, mercurial temperament.

Michael O'Byrne, also below medium height, had dark wavy hair, and, at the age of thirty-three, was already starting to run to fat. He was the archetypal Belfast man, a product of Divis.

Kelly's origin lay in Dungannon, Co. Tyrone, ten miles inside the mockery known as the Ulster border, deep in 'Bandit Country' where Republicanism held sway. Slim and above average height, with thinning brown hair belying his twenty-two years, he was imbued with the drive of the zealot, and was therefore—the youngest of them—regarded as the leader.

Twenty minutes later they were parked up just off Finsbury Square and walking towards Liverpool Street station, Kelly carrying a partly filled plastic carrier bag under his right arm while his left hand was thrust deep into his raincoat pocket. Naturally left-handed, he was holding the concealed revolver.

The plastic bag placed in the Polyfoto box, they returned to the Cortina and drove off up the City Road, taking the long way round to Chelsea Bridge.

Two

Big Ben ticked on impassively, as the Range Rover, its blue lamps flashing, sirens screeching and headlamps blazing, shot eastwards over Westminster Bridge. The massive landmark, towering above the Palace of Westminster, had only just finished shattering the early morning calm with its noisy sequence of full chimes and seven sonorous notes, only slightly muffled by the frosty fog swirling around the river area.

The traffic on the bridge—light at this time of the morning—gave way reluctantly, in response to the demands of the lamps and sirens, as PC Clem Jones accelerated to the safe speed imposed by the combination of reduced visibility and icy road surface. Leaving behind the stone lion at the eastern end of the bridge, Jones braked skilfully as he sped towards the roundabout, then accelerated past a helpful taxi-cab, whose driver waved him on his way into York Road. He just avoided a pedestrian, startled in mid-step and hovering on the start of the zebra crossing, on his somnambulant way to the paper factory known to the world at large as County Hall.

'Dozy sod!' grunted the shadowy figure in the passenger seat, dismissing this fleeting hazard as he studied the street map, checking the best route to Greenwich. This was Major Andrew Johnston, a retired army expert, now a civilian police explosives officer, hurrying towards the job that they all dreaded. Johnston, his driver and their vehicle formed a team known as Bomb Two.

Just before seven o'clock, arriving at his office and picking up the telephone handset, he had heard the sickening message: 'Sergeant James, Information Room here. There has been an explosion at Royal Naval College, Greenwich, and an explosives officer has been seriously injured. I'm afraid that we've got no further information but we're trying to find out more details. This message is timed at 06.55. Who is that, please?'

'Bomb Two. I'm on my way.' Reaching for the sheaf of messages hanging from a clip on the wall at his side, Johnston switched on the intercom and called to his driver in the kitchen, 'Forget the tea! We've got one, Clem. On the lamp!'

The Royal Naval College, steeped in history, was a prestige terrorist target. Built in 1705, to Sir Christopher Wren's design, as the Greenwich Hospital, for aged and disabled naval ratings, its role was changed in 1873 to its current one of training naval officers for higher professional qualifications, in addition housing the official residence of the First Sea Lord.

The last message on the clip, timed at 05.58, confirmed that a suspect bomb had been found at the College and that the night-duty man, Joe Hawke, had gone to the scene.

Easing over into the centre of the road, Clem Jones concentrated on working up the best speed, changing up with practised ease, only to be forced down again as pedestrians, heavy-eyed and comatose from their train journeys, emerged from the shadows to perform their individual evasion tactics on the crossing leading from Waterloo Station to the Shell building. Successfully negotiating this human skittle alley, the Range Rover shot under the railway bridge and into the Waterloo Road roundabout.

'Stamford Street!' shouted Andrew Johnston above the engine noise. The Range Rover slid sideways under the nose of a desperately braking double-decker bus, with Clem Jones trying to impose his will on the elderly driver of a slow-moving, rust-disfigured yellow Austin 1100 which had appeared on the outside track, cocooned in a world of his own. Leaving the old man to recover from his near heart attack while staring, sweating and trembling, at the low wall which surrounded the sunken area in the centre of the roundabout, Bomb Two weaved its way commandingly across a thin stream of traffic coming off Waterloo Bridge, then turned left into Stamford Street.

The radio burst abruptly into life. It had been totally silent for some time, as if the rest of the working world had suspended operations, as if there was no crime any more. 'Bomb Two from Control. State location and ETA at Greenwich. Traffic build-up in the area intensifying. Over.'

Johnston picked up the handset and pressed the switch. 'Bomb Two to Control. Now in Stamford Street. ETA Greenwich, ten to fifteen minutes, one-zero to one-five minutes. Propose arrival at West Gate. Over.'

Replacing the handset, he reached into the paper bag which occupied the well on top of the fascia and extracted a boiled sweet which he slipped into his mouth. As ever, he resolved to suck it to the end, but it didn't always work out that way.

Its accelerating engine roaring, with the echo of sirens beating back off the buildings on each side of the road, Bomb Two made good time until, as they were approaching the IPC building, a pedal cyclist drowsily swayed out of Hatfields on the near side, wobbled briefly, and then fell sideways in a clattering, undignified heap.

Assessing their chances in a flash, Clem Jones took a split-second decision and drove, with all lights ablaze, on the right hand side of the small island in the centre of the road. On the wrong side now, his vehicle doing better than fifty miles an hour, Andrew Johnston glanced up to see an enormous TIR articulated lorry bearing menacingly down on them through the fog, hissing and snorting under the influence of hastily applied brakes. Stamping his foot on an imaginary brake, he tightened his grip on the fascia just in time to wedge himself in as Clem Jones, with consummate artistry, swung the vehicle back on to the left-hand side of the road, slipping past the now stationary lorry to slot neatly into a narrow gap which had appeared between a large blue van and a small red car, to the fright of its driver.

Ryan Kelly stepped from the call box at the Battersea Park end of Chelsea Bridge where he had just finished telephoning the Liverpool Street bomb threat to the London Transport headquarters. He had dropped off here while his two companions went on to dump the car in Chelsea as part of a ploy to confuse any subsequent police investigation. In accordance with her instructions the telephone operator had done her best to prolong the conversation but he understood quite well what she was up to, and had cut her off as soon as he had finished passing the message.

A member of a new Active Service Unit operating in London and the southern Home Counties, he had nevertheless taken part in many terrorist acts in his native Tyrone. He was now only a short walk from the top floor flat which he shared with Michael O'Byrne and would be sound asleep before the other terrorist came in.

As he was walking warily through the fog by the Battersea Dogs' Home, members of a completely different independent unit were setting up two 'spectaculars' in nearby target areas.

Padrig Coyle—apparently engaged in a study of the thin dribble of traffic crossing the bridge—leaned back against the railing on the up-river side of Vauxhall Bridge, his right hand thrust casually into his raincoat pocket. Almost completely hidden in the shadow of a large granite block he was, in fact, the look-out man covering Tom Walsh, and the hand in his pocket was firmly gripping a cocked .357 magnum revolver. One of a family of committed 'freedom fighters' from County Kerry in the Republic, he was of medium height, lean but muscularly built, his pale face surmounted by a shock of thick black hair. Restless, itchy, his nerves were twanging because he lacked the means of communicating with Walsh. He preferred to have the company of others.

Tom Walsh was a half-Irish Londoner who had spent six years in the RAF Regiment, where he had learned to handle explosives and weapons, and had grown to hate the English with the smouldering passion of the expatriate semi-Celt, raised on half-truths and mystical romance. He was engaged in the final disposition and linking-up of a black mass wedged between the girders under the bridge—a job demanding his full concentration. A job to be completed in total silence, mostly in the dark, using his sense of touch and all of his experience.

A low whistle told Coyle that Walsh was now on his way up, the job finished, and after a short delay the bomber slid over the top of the railing to join him. Pausing only for Walsh to put on an RAF raincoat which he had secreted nearby, they moved off towards Vauxhall Cross, conversing in low tones. Directly ahead of them as they went down the subway leading to the underground station they could see the headlights of a saloon car drawing to a halt under the railway bridge in Lambeth Place. That would be Bren and Sean. They did not stay to watch them. Time: 07.25.

The grey and green Consort had been driven warily through the freezing gloom over Lambeth Bridge, along Albert Embankment and into the Vauxhall Cross one-way system. As it turned into Lambeth Place the two occupants could see a No. 77 bus, unlit and silent, standing at the bus stop, its cooling engine ticking. There was no sign of its crew, so Brendan O'Loughlin eased the offside wheels over the kerb trying to get as near as possible to the wall. His companion, Sean McAllister, tensed by inactivity, gave vent to an explosive profanity as the car's rear end swung sharply away when Brendan applied the footbrake. Water running down the wall and on to the paving slabs had frozen into a thin film of ice, hard to distinguish in the gloom.

O'Loughlin twisted around in his seat and reached back to a small box lying on the rear seat. After a struggle, he managed, with his left hand, to tease out a wooden dowel from a hole in the box's side, making use of a wire loop at the end of the dowel which he pocketed.

McAllister was, by now, standing beside the car, wound up, his head turning from side to side, his right hand thrust deep into a pocket in his heavy, navy-blue working jacket. If he had tried to look suspicious, he could not have improved on his performance. A short, thick-set, bearded, unkempt product of a Glasgow slum tenement, his scruffy appearance was in marked contrast to the other members of his ASU. His addiction to strong liquor, his stupidity and his abrasive behaviour were becoming a liability to the group. All too often his reactions were comparable with those of a cornered rattlesnake. He nursed an outsize inferiority complex, but carrying the heavy .45 automatic and a spare magazine always did something for his ego.

O'Loughlin slid out of the driver's door, closing it behind him, and eased himself forward between the front wing and the glistening fetid wall. Intelligent, good-looking, a convinced Marxist, he was a born organiser and highly disciplined; his companion he found crude and dangerously unpredictable. 'Come away, Sean, it's running now. For Christ's sake take your hand out of your pocket—you're so bloody obvious! Let's get down to the train. Once we're on it, we're not together, understand? It's the best way. We can keep an eye on each other and still not look like we're together.'

Releasing his hold on the automatic, McAllister followed with an ill-tempered grunt. It was a waste of time saying anything anyway—he never won. He would be bloody glad when he could get out of this team and back over to Belfast—plenty of shooting over there even if it was only knee-capping. And plenty of drink too!

As they walked steadily towards the subway leading down to the underground station, the soft wire on the end of the clothes peg in the box stretched inexorably, allowing the contacts on the other end to move towards each other and finally arm the large bomb in the car.

* * *

Speeding across the closed entrance to Rotherhithe Tunnel, Clem Jones aimed the vehicle into Lower Road, and settled down for the last two and a half miles of comparatively straight road. Weather conditions worsened as they got closer to the river's edge. Outside, it was bitterly cold, the deepening fog obscuring the parked cars, crouched glistening under a layer of frost, while the windscreen wipers were beginning to labour in their work, despite the heater going full blast.

With its tyres brushing the kerb on a slight left-hand bend as it headed towards Creek Bridge, Bomb Two dived into a thicker band of fog which concealed a sheet of black ice overlying the road surface. As the front wheel struck a small obstruction in the gutter, the Range Rover took on a life of its own, revelling in the forty-mile-an-hour spinning skid. His vision through the windscreen obscured, with lights flashing by in a frenzied jumble, Johnston desperately tightened his grip on the fascia, thrusting himself back into his big seat and jamming his feet deep into the seat well. A loose book on top of the fascia slid, like a rocket, in Clem Jones's direction but its movement was arrested by Johnston's well-timed right-handed catch. Clem, after all, was fully engaged, yet again, in justifying the confidence of his instructors in grading him as Class 1—the ultimate accolade in the world of driving.

Turning the wheels into the skid, Clem braced himself in his seat, his powerful hands clamped, vice-like, on the steering wheel, and thrust his left foot on the clutch pedal, simultaneously easing his right from the accelerator. Totally committed to his fight against the spinning skid, he concentrated on keeping the vehicle upright—if it rolled, that would be curtains for both of them. Time seemed to pass in slow motion, with all his strength engaged in the tension of the desperate struggle to regain control.

Running abruptly off the edge of the ice sheet, the wheels once more regained their grip, enabling him to bring the vehicle to a halt, across the centre of the road, its bodywork giving a final muted shudder, protesting against its loss of temporary freedom. Momentary reaction against the narrowness of their escape was dismissed by Clem Jones's faintly ironic, 'Here endeth the lesson! And some other bugger was reading it!' Which was followed by a 'Well done, you bloody lunatic bootneck!' uttered with feeling from the passenger seat.

Another sweet made its way into Andrew Johnston's mouth — the fifth so far and not one had completed its full term. Clem Jones accepted one without comment and, slipping the engine once more into gear, drew away. Tension was dispelled finally, in the short term at least, after a none-too-silent gear change, by a faintly mocking 'Hendon-trained!' from Johnston, answered by an appropriate two-syllabled rejoinder.

Two minutes more saw Bomb Two over the rise of Creek Bridge, through the one-way circuit under the shadow of the *Cutty Sark's* frost-rimmed rigging, and drawing up at the West Gate, where the MOD constable on duty pointed to the Met inspector standing farther along the internal road near the end of the seamen's hospital grounds.

Coming up to him, Andrew Johnston made a mental note of the time—07.18—and was so startled that he rechecked it straight away. Surely it had taken more than sixteen minutes? More than six miles, through fog, on icy roads, with at least one determined look into the abyss—it was unreal but undeniable. Telling Clem to inform Control that they had arrived, he turned his attention to the heavily built, uniformed figure standing at the side of the vehicle.

The 7.15 a.m. from Southend Victoria to Liverpool Street pulled into Rayleigh station with a squeal of brakes. The carriage doors rumbled back into their recesses, letting in the freezing air and rousing the thin scattering of shivering commuters from their misery. Silently, like automata, they stepped into the carriages and made for the seats, while the doors rattled shut. The explosive hiss of air escaping from the hydraulic brakes was followed by a jerky take-off as the train left the station, its speed building up rapidly.

In the distinctly open plan interior of the third carriage, much of the heat having fled through the open doors at the station, Sid Higgins sat hunched in a corner seat, trying desperately to restore some body warmth. A messenger with a city merchant bank, he wore the trousers and shirt of his working uniform topped by a sports jacket and shabby raincoat, the neck of which was sealed by a tartan woollen scarf. Three years short of the minimum retirement age he spent most of his time looking forward to the days when he would no longer need to leave his pre-war semi in weather like this.

In the police lodge, where welcome mugs of tea were forthcoming, Johnston studied the duty Met inspector. Just above minimum height, balding head haloed by a fringe of blond hair, inclined to portliness, he exuded an air of calm efficiency. He explained to Johnston all that had happened from the time that he had learned of the coded bomb warning.

Johnston interrupted the recital. 'Was the area lit? Did you use a torch? Did the bag look full?'

'No, the area wasn't lit, so I shone my torch from halfway up the steps. I'm not sure of the colour but the bag was certainly dark, plain — not tartan.'

'Did you get the impression that anybody might be hanging around? Perhaps down by the river or in a car on the main road? By one of the other buildings? What I'm wondering about is the chance of a remote control device, and particularly a second one which may still be in position.'

'No.' The word was drawn out and accompanied by a shake of the head. Obviously searching his memory and treating the question very seriously, the inspector continued, 'I can't say that I did, but it was pretty dark around there then—even without the fog.' He paused briefly, and then went on, 'I started to set up the cordon—our troops were just starting to arrive—along the perimeter fence, leaving out the hospital. I hadn't got enough blokes to cover the river wall so

I decided to ignore it—something had to go until we could get more men. What with the fog and the size of this place anybody could have been wandering around, let alone hiding. What was the other question? Oh, yes, the bag looked about half full, if that helps.'

A constable poked his head around the door. 'Your chief superintendent's just arriving, sir.'

On his way to the door, the inspector explained, 'He's been to the hospital—went direct from home—should have the latest on Joe Hawke, though, from what I saw earlier, it's not going to be particularly good.'

Johnston cut in quickly. 'Before we see the great man—have you had any chance to look for a second device?'

The inspector shook his head.

The silver-braided cap moving into the pool of light by the door announced the arrival of Chief Superintendent Marvell, Metropolitan Police. Barely acknowledging the inspector's presence, he addressed Johnston. 'Your man, Hawke, is in intensive care. Broken arm, some lung damage suspected, deep wound under his eye—his helmet saved him from further head injuries, they say—and a thigh wound near the femoral artery, right leg. He was lucky! He's still unconscious, so there's been no chance to get a statement from him.' This last sentence was uttered as if Joe had been deliberately withholding information.

Andrew Johnston, who had met him previously and was not impressed, was well aware of his contempt for civilian staff, and accepted the information without comment. Why waste his breath?

Marvell made a preliminary move in the direction of the King's Entrance, continuing: 'Well, Mr Johnston, if you are ready, we'll go down and have a look at the scene.'

Without moving, Johnston replied, '*We* will not be going anywhere near the scene, Chief Superintendent. The approved procedure is that, until *I* am satisfied that the area is completely safe, nobody else will be allowed inside the cordon. Until *all* explosive hazard has been eliminated, this is my scene, I'm afraid.' Turning back to the inspector, he went on, 'There are still some important points to be cleared. What time did Joe Hawke arrive? What time was the explosion? Is there any information about the Bomb Squad arriving? And what about the press?'

'He arrived at 06.15 and the explosion was heard at 06.40. Bomb Squad should be there at any time now—they were called some time ago. The press have started to arrive and you can bet on Radio London and LBC sending their people—that's one of the things that has to be covered—we'll have to put them somewhere. Press Bureau has, of course, been put in the picture.'

Checking with his watch, Andrew Johnston saw that the time was 07.35—the stand-off period before any further investigation could be undertaken would need to run for at least another five minutes. He turned again to the Chief Superintendent. Smiling, he said, 'I wonder if we can have another cordon set up along the other side of King William Walk—they will have to find somewhere else for the bus stop—and do our best to keep the Maritime Museum grounds clear. I'm rather concerned about the possible use of telephoto lenses when the light is good enough. I am sure that you know about the agreement not to photograph us or the Bomb Squad. That's pretty well established with the responsible part of the press, but there's always some clever sod out for easy money!'

With a grunt, the Chief Superintendent moved off to set the wheels in motion, and Johnston went with the inspector to the Range Rover where Clem Jones was manning the radio. Johnston opened the nearside door, took off his jacket, placed it on the seat, then, reaching inside, lifted his bomb jacket from its parking place and struggled into it. Clem indicated that there were no calls and then, unasked, passed out Andrew's helmet, personal radio and high-intensity lamp.

Putting on his helmet, Andrew Johnston settled it comfortably in position, and said to the inspector, 'I'm going up to have a look. When the Bomb Squad arrive, keep them here, please, and put them in the picture. The problem could still be a radio-controlled ambush bomb and I don't want anybody wandering into danger. If somebody else gets hurt the shit really will be in the fan and Captain Bloody Marvell will be upstairs collecting fares at the time.'

His weatherproof jacket now on, his tools stowed in its pockets, he turned away and made off towards the scene of the explosion, testing his personal radio after a few steps. With the time now 07.40, hints of daylight could be sensed rather than seen through the foggy darkness. Pausing by the tennis courts, their chain-link fence dripping with moisture, he switched on his lamp, playing its piercingly strong beam over the faces of King Charles Building on his left, and King William Building on his right.

Dimly visible through the poor light, the buildings loomed menacingly over him as he moved between them down the centre of College Road, his senses sharply tuned, his lamp beam probing every shadow. Reaching the end of King Charles Building he turned left, presenting his back to the scene of the explosion; then, keeping close to the flower beds in the centre of Grand Square, he made his way towards the river and across the square, by means of a central walk, to play his light over the façade of Queen Anne Building.

Concentrating totally on the moving patch of light as it fought its way through the thick fog, he carefully checked the building frontages towards the East Gate, his stomach muscles tensing sickeningly at the sight of a paper carrier bag lying, crumpled, in a low doorway. Closer investigation, occupying several minutes, eliminated the bag, and letting out a long, shuddering breath, he turned back to the steps leading up to the Queen's Entrance at the corner of Queen Mary Building.

Inch by inch, observing every precaution, he climbed the steps, checking slowly and exhaustively, until he reached the elevated portico, a mirror image of the one in which the explosion was said to have occurred.

Farther along the road, he came to a very broad flight of

stone steps, leading up to Upper Grand Square, a raised expanse of paving, bounded on both sides by tall, perfectly proportioned stone columns marching elegantly away through the fog.

Crouching at the centre of the top step, he played the brilliant beam from his lamp over the silent colonnades and the whole of the square. Finding nothing, with his concentration lessened, he became aware of the background noises which had not been registering with him since walking away from the Range Rover—the muted traffic noises, the grunt and growl of fog-horns struggling dyspeptically to send their warnings to fog-bound shipping, the now well-advanced retreat of darkness, the lessening of the enveloping fog.

He became aware, too, of the steadily chilling film of thin sweat covering his body, bringing realisation that, steadily and secretly, tension had been building up in him during the search. Then, releasing a slow, deep, audible breath, he readied himself for the final part of his tour—the King's Entrance, with its aura of tragedy.

He was soon picking his way warily through the light debris which became more plentiful as he walked diagonally down the broad steps to the foot of those which led up to the bomb scene. The long-familiar flat smell of consumed high explosive, mingling with that of damp mortar, grew stronger as he mounted.

Pausing near the top of the steps, his attention was seized by the gaping hole directly in front of him, framed by the obscenity of pulverised stonework and the shattered remains of a pair of tall, polished, heavy wooden panelled doors and their massive wooden frames.

His mind switched to the possibility of a further menace—could this be a so-called 'come-on' situation in which the intended victim was attracted into a target area, to be mown down by a second device, either timed to detonate after a set interval or fired remotely by a hidden watcher? At least the sniper threat could be discounted in the present visibility.

Given the requirement that any second bomb would have to be portable, it wasn't likely to be particularly heavy or powerful so it would, therefore, be fairly close to the first or to the approach routes. It took Johnston several minutes of gut-tightening, detailed work, as far as possible from behind cover, to satisfy himself that nothing else had been planted in the area.

Returning to his examination of the scene of the explosion, he could see that the absence of any crater in the stone floor, the generally regular pattern of the damage to the doors and the spalling of the stone door surround all pointed to one conclusion. The device must have been hanging on the door about three feet up from the door-step and this view was reinforced by the damage to the inner wooden door and the small lobby in which it was set. The bag that the inspector had seen had without doubt contained the bomb, and he had done well to leave it alone.

In the areas on either side of the doorway two items stood out like beacons against their jumbled backgrounds—a number of shredded, blackened fragments of dark blue canvas lying at the bottom of the stone balustrade and, over to the left, near the corner of the colonnaded walk, a pool of drying blood. They indicated not only that the bomb had been concealed in the duffle bag, but that Joe Hawke had been turning the corner, approaching it, not actually dealing with it.

The possibilities ran through his mind: not anti-handling, not a 'dropper', not very likely to be proximity, possible remote control. Most probably ran out of time but it could have been light-sensitive—what torch was Joe Hawke carrying and where was it now? Examination of the debris, carefully collected and transferred to the laboratory, would tell the full story, but he had already got a fair idea of it.

With the Painted Hall inside, crowned by Sir James Thornhill's magnificent painted ceiling, this scene was going to need careful treatment. To gather evidence, while avoiding even the suspicion of unnecessary intrusion or damage, was going to need painstaking judgement to keep everybody happy.

Careful not to disturb the scene by trampling all over it—visiting officers could be relied upon to do that if they were not properly herded, the more senior the more likely—he went back down the steps and walked thoughtfully to the Range Rover, where he found the inspector, now in the company of a number of others. Prominent among them were a Bomb Squad inspector and the two dog-handlers, their eager charges wriggling ecstatically in anticipation. Time: 08.05.

Once Johnston had briefed them, the dog-handlers moved off, their dogs, feeling the tug of the leads and sensing that their part was about to start, cavorting around them like excited puppies. With the outside faces of the four main buildings, the perimeter and the car parks still to clear, they would be occupied for quite a while yet. Theirs was a deliberate, methodical and time-consuming task, potentially dangerous and not to be rushed. It was team-work in its purest form, the dog's questing nose, enthusiasm and intelligence culminating in one of a variety of visual signals when explosive was detected, while the handler—giving encouragement, its form tailored to suit his individual animal—had the ability to recognise his four-legged partner's message.

Turning back to the others, Johnston was in the middle of explaining that the damaged entrance was the one leading to the Painted Hall and that the search of the scene would require special treatment, when a messenger arrived to say that his office wanted to talk to him on the telephone and was hanging on. He hurried to the police lodge and picked up the handset to be told: 'There's a problem at Liverpool Street—a suspect carrier bag down in the Central Line tube station. The area has been evacuated, the duty officer is on the scene, and the railway people are getting jumpy. They're passing trains through without stopping.'

Johnston chewed his lip. 'Who else is available?'

'Bomb Five. Bomb Nine is sick. His wife's just phoned

in—gastric flu—he's been giving us the shits for long enough, it's his turn now. There's nobody else until midday.'

'OK. I've pretty well cleared this scene for safety so I can leave, but somebody will have to carry on here, or it will have to wait until I can get back. Always assuming that nothing else turns up. Where is Bomb Five now?'

'He's not here yet—still on his way in from Caterham, I expect. I heard from him before he left, about half an hour ago.'

'Fair enough. Call him over the air and divert him—he can take over.'

Walking towards his Range Rover through the raw, patchy fog, Johnston made a circular motion with his right hand to tell Clem Jones that, once again, they would soon be on the move. Pausing to update the Bomb Squad officer and the inspector, he returned his helmet, lamp and radio to their stowage places; then, throwing his jacket into the back of the vehicle, he climbed back into his seat, picked up his clipboard, and rapidly prepared a brief summary of the situation, emphasising the important features, and asked the duty officer to make sure that it was given to Bomb Five when he arrived.

Sid Higgins shivered as he left the train at Stratford, fifteen minutes late because of the weather, the cold wind biting through his inadequate clothing and the fog striking rawly against his face, transforming his nose into a frigid, unfeeling appendage. Every day of his commuting life, he, like thousands of others, changed at Stratford, transferring to the Central Line underground train. Compared with the route march that would be involved at Liverpool Street—along the platform, down the stairs and tunnels, then down the escalator and on to the train—changing at Stratford was simplicity itself. All he had to do was cross from one side of the platform to the other.

But today, as he did so, there was a notice in the centre of the platform. Hastily scrawled in yellow chalk on a piece of black-painted hardboard, it advised passengers that trains were not stopping at Liverpool Street but would be passing through to the Bank. Committed normally to changing to the Circle Line at Liverpool Street on his way to Mansion House, he would have to sort out an alternative route. The Southend train was already pulling out so there was no way that he could get to work on time.

Three

'Bomb Two to Control. Leaving Greenwich for Bishopsgate via Blackwall Tunnel. ETA one-five to two-zero minutes. Over.'

'Received, Bomb Two. Your message timed at 08.15. Control out.'

Swinging left out of the West Gate, the Range Rover accelerated along King William Way, then, with blue lamps and sirens working full blast, shot left across the zebra crossing into Romney Road, eastwards. Johnston experienced, as on many previous occasions, the mounting exhilaration that came with travelling at high speed with a highly efficient driver steering his way through a constantly varying set of circumstances set by totally unknown and mainly unpredictable personalities.

With Rotherhithe Tunnel now closed for repairs and renovation, Blackwall was the obvious choice, the bridges being too far in one direction, and Woolwich Ferry too far in the other. Heavy frost still held the metropolis in its iron grip but the fog was hesitating, trying to decide its next move. Traffic was building up now and the morning rush hour was well established, many of the drivers only just now hearing about the incident as they listened to the news programmes and chat shows on the car radios.

Bomb Two wound its way down the old approach road, then up the short ramp to feed diagonally right-handed into the new motorway tunnel approach. This was probably the period of heaviest traffic movement through the tunnel and Clem Jones was forced to use every ounce of driving skill to weave his way through several packed lanes of vehicles, all jockeying for position, before squeezing into two lanes at the entrance.

Glancing to the right, across to the gasworks, Johnston's thoughts turned back, momentarily, to that night in January 1979, when the whole area was flooded with Inferno-esque light from more than a million cubic feet of gas ignited by a terrorist bomb, blazing away like a beacon of living, furious flame. How many people, including those on the 'job', he wondered, appreciated that, had it not been for the earlier conversion to North Sea Gas, that incident, which had given birth to the biggest fire in the locality since the Second World War, would have ended in massive destruction after a cataclysmic explosion? The *en masse* explosion of that amount of town gas, mixing with air, would have produced a fire ball to lay waste all the surrounding area.

Johnston pressed the transmit switch. 'Control from Bomb Two. Now entering Blackwall Tunnel and switching off. Over.'

This message was necessary to indicate to Control that they would be out of contact until they had surfaced, over a mile farther on, on the northern bank of the river. He followed Control's acknowledgement with a number of actions: switch off radio, close all windows, switch off blower, close off ventilators. The deeper one penetrated into the tunnel the greater the concentration of foul exhaust fumes; it is one thing to watch the air becoming bluer outside but quite another to suck the poison into your travelling box deliberately.

Each keeping to his own pavement, the two car-bombers were walking northwards along Edgware Road. When the Victoria Line train arrived at Vauxhall, they had boarded separate carriages—a convenient arrangement, with the Glaswegian a compulsive cigarette addict in contrast to O'Loughlin's dislike of the weed. It wasn't that he did not enjoy smoking—he had never tried it. There was no way that he could allow any outside influence—be it alcohol, drugs or nicotine—to breach his chilling self-control.

Their watchful separation was maintained without difficulty to Oxford Circus, through the change-over to the Central Line and then on to Marble Arch, where the planned get away route had involved returning again to frozen, foggy street level.

McAllister, shoulders hunched against the cold, slouched along, hugging the shop fronts, a picture of sullen misery, with both hands thrust into his jacket pockets. The combined effects of anti-climax, now that the car-bomb was in position, and his solitary journey, linked with the knowledge that it would be more than an hour before the pubs opened, were further exacerbating his misanthropic tendencies.

The sound of a bus approaching from behind and swooping in towards the bus stop just short of Praed Street, some eighty yards ahead, attracted his attention and, glancing up, he saw it was the No. 16 that he had been told to take for Brondesbury station. Discarding the half-smoked cigarette that had been drooping from his mouth, he broke into a sprint in an attempt to catch up with the bus. It was the action that he had been craving, but as he ran along the narrow pavement, hemmed in by kerb-edge railings, he was halted by a metallic clatter from near his feet. The spare magazine, dislodged when he took his hands from his pockets, fell to the pavement and bounced noisily away.

From his position across the road, O'Loughlin stepped into a shop doorway as if sheltering from the weather and stood immobile, watching. Powerless to change the course of events, he could already divine the outcome. From that moment, McAllister, written off, was on his own. The military dictum of never reinforcing failure had been well learned.

A passer-by, skilfully trapping the skittering object with his foot, stopped and was bending down to retrieve it when, in mid-movement, comprehension flooded in, only to be overshadowed by the harsh, aggressive voice snarling, 'Leave the bloody thing alone, ye bloody English bastard!'

McAllister, his rancour now having burst its bounds, was facing him in a crouch, the heavy automatic gripped waist-high in a white-knuckled hand and pointing at the unfortunate man as he slowly straightened up. Like the weapon he was holding, he was fully cocked and the slightest pressure on his trigger would precipitate disaster. In that restricted, frozen, open-air set, the players stood transfixed until a scream from a middle-aged woman speared the air.

Stooping swiftly, the gunman snatched up the loaded magazine, muffing the first grab through nerves and frozen fingers, then backed up against the adjoining wall, his gun moving from side to side, threatening the small spellbound crowd.

'Any one of ye tries to be a bloody hero gets bloody shot. And that goes for anybody who looks like he's following me!'

Spinning round, he vanished into a narrow side-street, heading for the anonymity of Paddington Station, more dangerous than ever now that he was a fugitive.

Brendan O'Loughlin crossed the road farther on and took his place, calmly and unobtrusively, in the bus queue waiting for the next No. 16.

Clem concentrated once more on the battle of wills—trying to force the cars and vans from the outside lane into spaces between the unending stream of heavies almost nose-to-tail in the other. A difficult task in the best of circumstances and not helped by members of the 'just one more' club—drivers compelled to assert their virility by passing just one more vehicle before making any attempt to yield. The siren's alternating scream was beating back from every surface in the tunnel, and the impression of speed was further accentuated by the steady downhill slope and the wet road glistening in the reflected lights.

A quick flash of subdued daylight came down an overhead ventilation shaft, and then a left hand dog-leg fed them into the level section of the tunnel, immediately under the river bed. A further quarter of a mile through the thickening blue haze, another ventilation shaft, and a right turn brought them to the final climbing stretch, with its view of the tunnel exit. Fighting against impatience, with no chance of improving their position in the queue, they crept up the slope into the open air between the dirty grey-green walls of the concrete canyon, and, moving across into the nearside lane, eased out leftwards up the ramp and into East India Dock Road. Johnston reported back on the air to Control as they sped westwards.

One of the busiest roads into the City at this time of the morning, this section of the A13 from Southend and Tilbury was jam-packed with traffic. Nevertheless, getting into his stride once more, it took Clem Jones only a few minutes to negotiate the mile to Limehouse, now less than ever like its mysterious, fictional fan-tan playing, opium-den image.

Here, at a confluence of six roads leading into a bottle-neck as the road curved around Limehouse Parish Church, they found traffic conditions officially described in Traffic Control parlance as 'black'—nothing moving. Clem inched his way through, bullying the other drivers into creating space which they would have sworn did not exist, even persuading some that a short spell on the pavement would go a long way towards getting rid of those insistent bloody two-tones.

Breaking out of the bottle-neck at last, Bomb Two accelerated away with Trafpol motorcyclists, normally committed to dealing with routine problems at the stage of the opening day, helping them on their way.

Brendan O'Loughlin got off the bus outside the narrow, seedy entrance to Brondesbury Station, which could hardly be described as one of the gems in British Rail's crown. During the twenty minutes' ride from Praed Street he had sat quietly just inside the bus where he could watch everybody boarding and alighting. Nobody had aroused his interest.

Walking around the corner, he entered a telephone box and dialled the number for the *Daily Express*. Speaking clearly, he made known the threat posed by the car bomb at Vauxhall, closing with the coded phrase included in messages from the Provisional IRA. As the voice at the other end of the line began to ask questions, he cut off the call sharply and left the box.

He then bought a ticket and climbed the stairs to the platforms. Finding that he had some time to wait before the arrival of his train to Canonbury, even though he was confident that he had nothing to worry about, he took up a position from which he could see the whole of the platform. It was not in his character to leave anything to chance if he could avoid it.

Clem Jones finally brought the Range Rover to a halt at the kerbside outside the booking hall of Liverpool Street Station, where an impassive sergeant of the City Police was waiting. Andrew Johnston opened his door, swung his legs out sideways, and stepped out on to the pavement beside the sergeant, his nostrils assailed by that peculiarly sour smell that seems to pervade all railway stations. The cold, raw atmosphere enveloped him within seconds and he was happy to put on his weatherproof jacket over the bomb jacket that he was still wearing. Ahead of him Post Office vans carried on delivering and loading mail bags at the collecting area without interruption, while taxi-cabs continued to ply their trade at the pavement's edge, putting down and lifting passengers as if no emergency existed.

Sensing Johnston's puzzlement, the sergeant, every inch an ex-guardsman, his height emphasised by the unique City helmet, with its numbered black and gold helmet plate, explained, 'The bomb's down in the Central Line booking hall, sir. The quickest way down would be by the steps through there—' he pointed behind the Range Rover—'but the duty officer is over the other side. He thinks that it's a better place to work from because those stairs lead directly down into the hall without any protection. We've taped off the area to keep everybody away from the stairs.'

Like all the other London main-line stations, Liverpool Street sustained two differing levels of activity. Long-distance trains from East Anglia, including Harwich boat trains and suburban commuter trains, all fed in and out of it, their peak-hour passenger totals reaching hundreds of thousands. An additional burden was presented by travellers arriving on the Central and other lines of London's Underground. A bomb incident there was about as welcome as an Income Tax demand.

Looking back, Andrew Johnston could now see a length of white tape which blocked off the area at the head of the stairs but still gave vehicles room to turn at the bottom of the ramp.

The sergeant continued, 'It was decided to keep the situation low key, as far as possible, until you arrived, but we can stop the traffic and clear this area pretty quickly if you want to. I'll show you the way across, sir, when you're ready.'

Clem Jones, meanwhile, had reported their arrival to Control and had handed helmet, lamp and radio to Johnston who now observed, 'I'll need my black bag and the spotter 'scope as well for this one, Clem.'

When these had been brought out from their stowage positions, the sergeant picked up the bag and they moved off through the glass doors into the booking hall, Johnston carrying his lamp, helmet and periscope. Time: 08.38.

Threading their way through the crowds in the hall, they moved over to the right and exited through a similar pair of doors, then made their way around the buffers standing resolutely at the end of the unoccupied line beside Platform 9, and into a short low tunnel, to turn left along a passageway leading to the chemist's miniature shop where a small knot of people waited beside the white tape which blocked the way forward.

One of them greeted Johnston. 'I'm John Richards, duty officer at Bishopsgate. Thanks for getting here so quickly, Major.' Indicating the man at his side, he continued, 'This is Barry Holmes. He'd better put you in the picture—after all it's his manor.'

This double act was a common feature of incidents at major railway stations—two teams for the price of one. British Transport were on their own ground but, invariably, called for the locals, in this case the City of London Police. At least with this particular combination it was easy to distinguish between them—the chrome or silver embellishments with blue-and-white diced bands around the caps of the BTP stood out against the City's combination of gold with red-and-white dicing.

Barry Holmes, also a uniformed inspector, took up the briefing. 'Our central Control, at Broadway, received a telephone threat, direct, about a bomb in a station—unspecified. Irish accent, but not coded. This was passed out for action at all main-line stations until we hit the jackpot—a plastic carrier bag dumped around the corner inside a Polyfoto box in the Central Line booking hall here. One of my chaps couldn't resist looking inside and nearly crapped himself. You can't tell some of them, particularly if they're young. Anyway, before he pulled out, he saw a large battery and some wires. At least he didn't touch them.'

'When was the threat received?' Johnston asked.

'At 07.10 and we passed the call to the Yard, saying we'd found it, at 07.45.'

'How have you secured the area? I presume the rest of the station has been checked?'

'Oh, yes, we've turned the rest of the station upside down and found nothing, so there's nothing to worry us there. Every way up and down from the Underground has been sealed off with tape like this one, all trains downstairs are being passed through without stopping and we've got a man on each Central Line platform just in case—they're railway staff. Everybody has been cleared from the booking hall and tunnels.'

During all this time the busy hustle and bustle of a main-line terminus went on but, even so, some of the commuters were finding time to hang around and spectate in spite of the cold—not that there was much to see at ground level. The media folk, of course, were quick to recognise this and, except for a look-out, inevitably the most junior, they were all ensconced in the comfort of the tea bar. Licensing hours were some way off yet, but expense accounts were already open.

'One last question,' said Johnston. 'What's the access route like?'

'Down these steps.' Holmes pointed to a metal grille drawn across the opening just past the chemist's and behind the fruiterer's. 'A tunnel leads down to the Bishopsgate tunnel and on to the booking hall. There's always the other way down of course, down the stairs from Platform 7, directly into the hall, but I thought that you would prefer the indirect route in . . . Will you be using your machine—what's it called?—"Wheelbarrow"?'

Johnston mentally blessed the Duty Officer's Bomb Course at Hendon, some of which had obviously stuck. 'Thanks, Barry, you're quite right about the approach route. I'd like the traffic completely stopped at the top of the ramp and the booking hall cleared—those glass doors worry me—and we've got to be absolutely certain that the area at the top of the other stairs is kept clear. I don't think this is a job for Wheelbarrow—it would take some time to set up and, anyway, we don't use it for every incident. Only when it's appropriate.'

The sergeant went off to organise the extra safety measures, taking a few helpers with him, and Johnston put a test call through to Clem Jones. The reception was not very good. No further calls had come in. Time: 08.45.

Johnston quickly put on a pair of rubberised gloves and then his helmet—it incorporated interior ear protectors against blast—and picked up the spotter 'scope and lamp. They went, together, down the steep steps. The steel nosing on these was highly polished by years of wear from millions of feet, so Andrew was circumspect in his descent. It wouldn't help anyone if he slipped arse over tip and broke something.

They turned into the Bishopsgate tunnel. The station noises

faded rapidly, and the only sounds were the companionable padding of their footsteps and the susurration of nylon against nylon coming from Andrew's weatherproof. The air was already appreciably warmer, with that peculiarly memorable taste of stale oil, dust and tombs.

Making their way forward, listening intently all the time, they quickly reached the start of an S-bend. Just beyond it, Holmes explained, was the Central Line booking hall. 'Then we'll stop here for a moment,' Johnston decided. He took out his radio and tried, unsuccessfully, to make contact with Clem Jones. After several attempts from different positions he abandoned his efforts, resigning himself to the fact that he had no radio link. 'What's the layout from here on?' he asked them. Once he was sure that he understood every detail of Holmes's description and had a clear picture of the booking hall and the position of the Polyfoto box, he said, 'I'd like you to move back a bit and be my link man. I'm going forward on my own—it's standard operating procedure—minimum risk and all that. It will help if I can be sure that my back-up is somebody that I can trust.'

Holmes backed off and Andrew Johnston, opening his black bag, took out his lightweight hook and line set, paid out the first thirty yards of line, laying it loosely on the ground, carefully avoiding any kinks, snags or tangles, and finished his preparations by unpacking and assembling his spotter 'scope on its tripod.

Once at the final part of the S-bend, he set up the 'scope so that he could look around the right-hand bend. Then he lay on the hard concrete, taking off his helmet and placing it within reach, so that he could study the booking hall in comfort. Looking down the slope he was disappointed to find that his view was confined to part of a booking office and a row of three old-fashioned telephone boxes against the back wall. Even using the 'scope he could see little of value, so he decided to change his position and so widen his field of vision.

Foraging once more in the black bag, he dug out a large

mirror on the end of a telescopic metal handle, and, with the line hooked on to the back of his jacket and carrying the mirror and lamp, he advanced slowly to the threshold of the booking hall.

As his concentration reached out with the questing intensity of radar beams, a tremor, travelling up through the floor and his boots and on to the soles of his feet, brought him to an immediate halt, tensed and listening, like a threatened animal poised for flight. One of the attributes of a live-explosives expert was the ability to judge when to run like hell and to blazes with everything else. The movement was followed almost instantaneously by a deep rumbling sound, then a surge of stale, warm, lifeless air told him that, far below, a train had passed through with its captive living cargo. At least that was going according to plan.

From Barry Holmes's briefing, he already knew that the Polyfoto box was concealed to the left of his route into the booking hall, so he would have to stop short to reduce any risk from that direction. Taking up a position on the right of the tunnel and then moving over to the left, he surveyed as much of the booking hall as he could, his heartbeats pumping loudly in his ears. His breathing quickened and his grip on the lamp tightened while he concentrated on a detailed, searching scrutiny of the area.

The hall was divided laterally with a barrier broken by several structures, two of them ticket offices, separated by two short rows of automatic ticket machines, their illuminated tops signalling that their mechanisms still waited, poised and eager, for their diet of coins. The ticket offices, together with the telephone boxes, formed most of a matching set, in early twentieth-century brown varnish, which was completed by a pair of ticket collector's shelters at the far end of the barrier.

On the other side of the barrier he could make out the upper end of three escalators, silent and immobile, their polished metal surfaces glistening under the overhead lights. The sound of another train rumbling through reminded him of the two men standing their lonely uninformed vigil below, their only contact with the world the periodic passage of brightly lit, jam-packed trains.

The wall to the right of the telephone boxes was pierced by the bottom flights of two sets of wide stone stairs, flanked on the far side by a small cigarette kiosk and, within touching distance of his observation post, by a larger bookstall-cum-tobacconist and sweet kiosk, still open but forlornly unattended.

The slow, deliberate search had not brought to light any obvious second device, but two problem areas still remained—the hidden places throughout the hall and, broodingly, silently threatening, the Polyfoto box, which he had still not been able to see. Standing his lamp on the ground, he pulled out the mirror handle to its fullest extent and adjusted the mirror on its universal joint to the best angle. Then, sheltering behind the left-hand wall, he poked the mirror forward, steadying it, so that he could at last have a sight of the box.

To his astonishment it was only about eight feet away, too near to be able to frame the whole of it in the mirror. He was forced to manoeuvre the mirror into a number of different positions in order to cover the structure piecemeal. A standard box of its type and function, it was about seven feet tall and three feet deep. Its curtained opening was out of view, pointing towards the ticket offices, so he had no chance of seeing inside from his present position.

During all the time that he had been below some part of his subconscious had been marshalling the facts, twisting them around, re-examining them, probing at the possibilities, trying to outguess the bomber . . . *Almost two hours since the threat . . . if it's a time-bomb it can't be worked by the minute hand—could be several hours left . . . Could, of course, be anti-disturbance . . . or light-sensitive . . . Couldn't establish a radio-link with Clem—too far underground—so it certainly isn't radio-controlled . . . Whatever the possibilities—one approach only, no chance at all of using Wheelbarrow*

. . . I don't know, though! Could carry Wheelbarrow down the steps . . . but that's another three-quarters of an hour and by then the bomb . . . No, not *Wheelbarrow . . .*

Closing up the mirror, he picked up the lamp and then realised that he would need two of the pulleys from his black bag, so went back and dug them out before returning to the entrance, picking up the 'scope on the way. Pausing to let Holmes know what he was up to, he gathered up all his gear and then, hesitating fractionally, stepped out from the protection of the tunnel to skirt the outer edges of the booking hall, trailing the line behind him like a foul-hooked fish. Reaching the ticket-collector's shelters, he unhooked the line and dumped his gear on one of the seats before moving over to the top of the right-hand escalator.

The northbound Victoria Line train drew into the platform at Green Park, and Tom Walsh, standing by one of the doors of a non-smoking carriage, pressed the red-rimmed button which triggered the door-opening mechanism. Stepping out on to the platform, he mingled with the peak crowd pushing its preoccupied way to work in offices, shops and businesses in the Piccadilly area of London's West End.

Seemingly unassociated with him, the black-haired Coyle emerged from the other door five yards to the rear but, unlike Walsh, failed to blend immediately into the crowd. As a Londoner, travelling by public transport was second nature to Walsh and he moved with easy confidence, but the Irishman stood out, subtly distinguishable from his fellows. With the hesitating, fearful air of someone travelling under memorised orders searching for confirmation by place names and directional signs, he gave the impression of a man following an unfamiliar path.

Trying to match the momentum of the throng whose main stream moved purposefully to the exits, Coyle moved along the platform, keeping his eye on Walsh, until the two of them edged into a small eddy following the signs to the Piccadilly Line.

Leaving the scene at Vauxhall behind them they had broken their journey at Victoria to gulp a greasy breakfast in a back-street café, before, attracted like moths to a flame, working their way back by a roundabout route through the fog to Millbank. Idling along the riverside, across the western end of Vauxhall, resisting the temptation to cross the river, passing into Grosvenor Road, they had kept their eyes about for any signs of police activity but had seen none.

Finding themselves, unexpectedly, at the entrance to Pimlico Gardens, a small green retreat at the river's edge, they had entered in the hope that it might provide a convenient observation point. But the fog had denied them any chance of studying the scene that they had left earlier.

Coyle broke the silence. 'What d'you think, Tommy? Have the bastards found them yet?'

'It's too soon yet, Paddy. They've not had time. Anyway, if they had found anything the whole bloody area would be blocked off by now and you'd be able to see the blue lamps and hear the noise a mile away. I don't reckon we should hang around here any longer—once they find the car they'll be stopping everybody they find and that could be aggravation.'

Slipping out of the gardens and across the road up past Dolphin Square, they had headed for Pimlico Underground station, boarding the train that was to bring them to Green Park.

The shivering, hunched figure in the dark blue Wimpey jacket climbed the steps leading from the platforms at Great Portland Street and crossed the road into Warren Street.

After the Praed Streed confrontation he had managed to reach Paddington Station, sweating with panic—a hair-trigger dangerous bundle of nerves. With no serious memory of the route that he had taken, the bustle and noise of the main-line station concourse came as surprise to him—a surprise that screwed up his tension another notch. With the instincts of a blind, crazed hare he jinked away from this obvious search area and out into the streets once more. Without pattern or plan to his movements he was, quite frankly, lost.

Heading unpredictably towards the canal bridge with the hand in his pocket now permanently locked on to the automatic, he finally hit Harrow Road. Unfortunately for him, he arrived at the under-and-over traffic interchange which served only to confuse him even further. Ten minutes later, at the corner of Harrow Road and Edgware Road, his heart stood still when he looked round to find that he was outside the modern police station. In no condition to absorb a shock like that, he shot down the subway to run blindly forward until he burst into the Underground booking hall.

Panting heavily, he fed coins into the most convenient ticket machine, snatched the ticket as it appeared and pushed blindly through the nearest gate. Seconds later he reached the platform—which one he did not know—then thrust his way through and joined a knot of people boarding the newly arrived train. Too wound up to consider sitting down, he positioned himself just inside the doors, to lurch, off-balance, as the train started off. Snatching at the overhead strap-hang, his eyes lighted on the long, narrow route map posted up over the sliding doors. Studying this, he found that he was travelling on the Circle Line, the easterly direction being confirmed when he glimpsed the name of the following station. He found it difficult to keep his balance, and suddenly realised that he was attracting too much attention. It unsettled him still further and he felt compelled to leave the train at the next stop which was Great Portland Street.

Scuttling blindly along Warren Street he felt that he was going roughly in the right direction, but the joint effects of almost continuous movement, sustained blind panic and the adverse weather, were mounting. It was no longer a question of if he would shoot, but when.

the black taxi drew up at the kerb in Tottenham Court

Road, its nearside door opened and Sid Higgins stepped out, turned to pay the fare and then pushed the door shut.

By good fortune the enforced change of plan at Stratford had not produced as many problems as he had feared and he had arrived at the bank only fifteen minutes late. The head messenger had brushed aside his explanation to tell him that as soon as he had changed into uniform there was an urgent delivery to be made.

Ten minutes later, in uniform and dark blue raincoat, Sid Higgins, a security document case chained to his left wrist, was hailing a taxi in the street outside, on his way to Warren Street.

Turning away from the paid-off taxi, he made to cross the wide pavement, his thoughts elsewhere, but was brought back to reality when the figure of McAllister, emerging from Warren Street, lurched into him.

Tightening his grip on his automatic, the Glaswegian snarled, 'Get out of my way, ye bloody Sassenach bastard, or I'll bloody make ye!'

Spinning around under the impact of the blow from McAllister's shoulder, Sid Higgins felt the document case slipping away and made a desperate grabbing attempt with his right hand to steady it. It was the last move he made, for McAllister, his befuddled brain interpreting it as a move for a hidden weapon, drew the .45, already cocked, to fire two shots at point-blank range.

Mortally wounded by the two heavy slugs, Higgins was driven back under their impact to sprawl in a pathetic heap on the pavement, a slowly spreading stain creeping out from under his crumpled body.

Four

Andrew Johnston walked briskly down the stationary escalator (never run with explosives around!) then, reaching the bottom, located each railway sentinel in turn to tell him to remain in position until signalled—even if there was an explosion. Climbing back up he decided to make use of the protection offered by the centre escalator for his next move, and transferred his lamp and 'scope to that position.

Setting up an operating position from which he could see into the Polyfoto box, he placed the lamp on the top, flattened, steps, lined it up with the opening, and then, going as far as possible down the unmoving ridged steps and into the cover of the side, he reached up and switched on the lamp. The beam of intense light shot across the gap into the opening, its power flooding the box's interior with a brilliance sufficient to trigger off any light-sensitive device that might be present.

There was no explosion, so, peering over the top, he placed the 'scope in position beside the lamp, and used it to study the opening. The edge of a white plastic carrier bag leaped into view, poking out from behind the left-hand upright, and the problems were now revealed. Several things needed to be accomplished at the same time—the bag had to be pulled out of position, upended and its contents tipped out on the ground in full view for further study and identification. If he was to do the job from behind cover he would need both pulleys in suitable positions.

With the lamp switched off, he moved over to the side of the barrier where he quickly set up the pulleys, before advancing on the Polyfoto box. Carefully reaching through the opening, he firmly engaged the hook in the bottom of the carrier bag, ignoring the attraction of its handles. Although using the handles appeared to be the obvious solution, they would be no help—he needed to do more than just move the carrier, he had to tumble it.

Then, slipping the line into the pulleys, he returned to the tunnel and placed all his equipment on the ground. Back now in the tunnel's protection he let out a long breath, the thumping of his heart sounding loudly in his ears. Picking up the coil of line on his way through, he moved back to where Barry Holmes had taken up position. Time: 09.20.

'Hello, Andrew. How's it going? I've been trying to follow your progress and work out what you've been up to by the sounds, but I couldn't hear a lot. Did you find it?'

'Oh, yes—*and* I've got a hook into it. Any time now and we'll be able to get a look at the thing.' He gave Holmes a brief summary of his activities and conclusions since they had last been together. He felt drained. For the last half-hour he had been immersed in a potentially dangerous situation, involved in a great deal of physical movement, totally exposed for some of the time, his thoughts wholly concentrated on that damned carrier bag.

Carefully, he took up the slack in the line, until he felt some resistance. With a word of warning to Barry Holmes, he jerked the line towards him and away from the booking hall. At first nothing happened as the line took up its inbuilt stretch, then as it gave towards him abruptly, he heard something clatter on to a hard surface in the distance. The sound was followed by a silence so intense that the thought flashed through Johnston's mind that there must have been an explosion, even though he could not remember it, and it must have shattered his ear-drums, leaving him stone-deaf. Then he became aware of the soft sound of Holmes letting out his breath in relief. The silence continued, as if the whole world, suspended in limbo, were peering over their shoulders, listening vainly for some further hint, some sign that life was still going on.

'I'll take a look at it,' Andrew said. 'But don't get impatient—even if that plastic bag turns out to be nothing I'm going to check the area for anything else that may have been left. I'll keep you posted as I go along.'

He set off once again as yet another rumble vibrated upwards from a passing train, triggering in his memory cells a conscious realisation that there had, in fact, been a steady stream of such sounds ever since he had tugged at the line, but they had failed to penetrate his concentration. Reaching the entrance of the booking hall once more, he picked up the mirror, extended the handle and, with its aid, was gratified to see that the contents of the carrier bag were now scattered over the floor in front of the Polyfoto box.

The battery and wires which the constable claimed to have seen were now revealed in their true role of a plant, a blind, a distraction, but the other objects shouted for attention. The main item was a bundle, some ten inches long and five in diameter, completely enveloped in dull black PVC, with two red-covered wires leading from a rectangular lump at one end to a wristwatch fixed to the centre of the bundle. Some screwed-up newspaper sheets and a Shredded Wheat packet lay nearby, while the carrier bag was suspended upside down from the hook near the first pulley. Fluttering slightly in the air rising up the escalators, it provided mute evidence that it had shed its entire contents.

Concentrating on the watch, Johnston tried desperately to get a view of its hands but was unable to create the right angle so, putting down the mirror, he went forward to get a better look at the device, calling back to let Barry Holmes know what he was doing. Bending down, he studied the bundle closely. The watch was not working, the sweep hand was present but motionless, the red wires were tucked under its back, but one of them had worked almost free. As he picked up the bundle the solid feel of wooden cylinders came through the tape wrapping. Time: 09.30.

With comprehension dawning, the pent-up tension of the situation tore through like a dam bursting under the pressure of a massive lake. A sodding hoax! Some bastard had caused all this bloody pantomime with a bloody hoax! The public inconvenience, the twitching nerves, just for this! Rising swiftly to his full height, Andrew Johnston raised the bundle as far as his right arm would allow, intent on smashing it to the floor. Then, years of training and experience re-established their control, and calmness and good sense flooded slowly back. Replacing the bundle carefully on the floor, he turned his attention to the Shredded Wheat packet.

This could, of course, be the real bomb, the one meant to take him out now that the hoax had drawn him into its orbit. Without moving the packet from its position on the floor, it was the work of only a few minutes, using his sharp knife, to establish that it contained nothing more lethal than its normal quota of fibrous, pillow-shaped bundles.

It had been a careful, deliberate hoax, the components of the false bomb arranged to make sure that anyone like himself would take all possible precautions and spend a great deal of time before discovering that it was harmless. He could not yet stop to worry about why anyone would have planted such an elaborate simulation of a lethal device—first he had to check the rest of the booking hall. He rapidly searched and cleared every potential hiding place—inside and on top of the Polyfoto box, the telephone boxes, every corner and shadowy area and then (although they must have been occupied at the relevant time) the cigarette kiosk, the bookstall, the booking offices and the ticket collectors' shelters. With the memory of earlier, more tragic, scenes returning, he paid particular attention to litter bins and their contents.

He shouted the news that it was now all clear to Barry Holmes, and then went through the barrier at the head of the escalators and called down to the look-outs on the platforms, telling them that they could relax.

Completing the clearing-up operations, Andrew Johnston recovered the carrier bag and its erstwhile contents and slipped them into a plastic bag to preserve them for further examination. Then, unzipping his weatherproof and bomb jacket to let in some air to his overheated body—his shirt and underwear were wringing wet with sweat, and distinctly uncomfortable—he sat for a few moments in the Polyfoto box, unwinding and considering the reasons for this hoax having been set up. It could of course have been done simply for its nuisance value; the terrorists had no compunction in the taking of human life, but might consider the disruption caused to the public sufficient in some cases to make their point, especially considering the man-power that the police, the railway and Underground staff, and people like himself were forced to waste. Or it could have been some total nut-case, with no cause beyond his own warped sense of amusement, who had . . . But then he remembered that the warning had been given in an Irish accent, and even though it had not been coded to indicate that it came from one of the recognised terrorist organisations, it seemed to him unlikely that it had been the work of some independent lunatic, particularly since it had been so convincingly arranged. No, it was almost certainly the work of one of the Irish groups, and the only question was whether it had been set up simply in order to cause maximum inconvenience, or whether there was some other motive—such as distraction of attention from other bombs . . .

There was really no point in speculation, but at least he felt calmer after the few moments of reflection. Barry Holmes joined him, offered his congratulations and helped him to recover the various pieces of equipment from their resting places. They walked back together through the tunnels and up the stairs, to the white tape. Time: 09.43.

Leaning against the wall in Highbury New Park, Brendan O'Loughlin covertly studied the area, together with any of the locals that came into view. His image was that of a man without a care, resting quietly and calmly before setting off once again. Satisfied that he was in the clear, he moved away, retracing his steps and turning into a side road in the Clissold Park area. Still taking precautions, he slipped into the doorway of a shabby Victorian terraced house. A traditional style with semi-basement and two other storeys, like many others in the locality it had been converted cheaply into three self-contained 'furnished' flats.

Standing in the privacy of the top floor flat he took off his anorak and placed it neatly on a hanger in the cheap wardrobe standing in the corner of the bedroom. One of a number of cheap conversions owned and rented out by a Pakistani landlord, it consisted of a sitting room, bedroom, kitchen and a crudely converted bathroom. The furniture was basic and strictly functional, with the exception of an old walnut-veneered, black-and-white television.

Busying himself in the kitchen, O'Loughlin considered the problem of McAllister's obvious demoralisation and panic. Sipping the instant coffee he had made, he reached out and switched on a small transistor radio standing on the draining board, but there was only music. Since leaving Praed Street he had heard nothing of McAllister's subsequent activities but, although he had left the scene quite deliberately in an operational decision of unusual detachment, O'Loughlin had not dismissed the problem out of mind.

As he saw it, the situation could come out in one of three ways. Mac could have escaped, or been caught, or killed, and each result would bring its own difficulties. If he managed to escape and find his way back, God knows who would be right behind him. If he was captured there was no knowing what the English police would get out of him. The third possibility might be best.

Going through to the sitting room, he took up position near the window with his Luger to hand, watching the road. Apart from the Glasgow buffoon, he was expecting a courier to bring in a fresh supply of the latest time and power units. They would make setting up bombs so much easier.

The freezing air and the daylight hit Johnston like a slap in the face. It should not have done, for the conditions were still virtually the same as when he went down, but he had been out of contact with the outside world for nearly an hour in a warm enclosed atmosphere, tensed, listening, concentrating but poised to duck, hide or run almost by reflex, should the need arise. Stepping into view at the top of the stairs, still partly preoccupied, he was startled to be the object of a spontaneous burst of applause from the small knot of spectators. It caused him to hesitate fractionally in mid-stride. Experience had prepared him for the whirr and click of cameras and bursts of light from flash-bulbs together with the shouted questions of the newsmen, but public applause of any kind was a pretty novel experience.

To the advancing John Richards he spat out, 'I suppose you've heard? It was a poxy bloody hoax!'

His helmet now held in his hand, he turned, his sweat-soaked hair feeling icy in the cold air, to thank Barry Holmes and hand the scene back to him formally. Complimenting him on his efforts, the inspector went off to search for the assistant station master so that the station could now be brought back completely to normal, above and below.

Recovering his personal radio from its pocket, Andrew Johnston pressed the transmit button and told Clem Jones to report the clearance and come on through to the station police office.

Standing in the office, Inspector Richards started to apologise for bringing him on a wild goose chase, but the Explosives Officer, taking off his weatherproof, broke in firmly with what was obviously a well practised speech, 'There's no need to reproach yourself—that's what they pay us for. Incidentally, there's no such thing as a hoax bomb, in spite of what the papers say!' Sensing Richards' surprise, he continued, 'What there *can* be is a suspect object which, after it has been properly checked out, proves to be a hoax. Very few people seem to want to understand that the job is just the same for us whether it's a live bomb, a hoax or a load of rubbish—until you have proved what it is. That's true whatever method you use—remote, the so-called "controlled explosion" or hand entry. The nervous build-up is just the same for every one, except perhaps in the remote method. The real trouble comes when some desk driver is looking at the figures—he's only interested in live ones—but we've got used to that. After you've been in this job for a while you come to accept that, for some jobs, a closed mind is a must.'

Turning to Barry Holmes, who had now reappeared, he said, 'It's up to you, I know, but I think this job ought to be treated as a crime—hoaxing is now a substantive offence—so I've worn gloves all the way through. Will you have it finger-printed? Can I leave it with you to have photographs taken? Then, if you want a statement from me, just ring my office.'

Finishing the coffee which had appeared, he settled down to the paper work in which every form of modern police work rapidly becomes enveloped. Sketches and descriptions were well under way when the telephone rang.

'Andrew, it's not your day,' said the voice of Detective-Sergeant Nigel Brockway. 'We've got a suspect car under one of the railway arches at Vauxhall Cross and a threat's been phoned to the *Daily Express*. The duty officer is at the scene, so they're clearing the area and stopping trains. How are you fixed? There's nobody else unless you want me to get one of the others in early, but you know how long that will take. Living as far out as they do, it'll be at least an hour before any of them can be operational.'

'Apart from the threat, what's the panic?'

'The position of the car for a start. Then the local law has looked inside and seen some wires coming from a box. It looks like a good shout. I reckon it's a blue lamp job.'

Nigel Brockway was young and occasionally given to assuming the dream role of master controller, and needed to be brought down to earth.

'Look—I'll decide whether or not we have the blue lamp flashing. I'm the silly bugger who'll be sitting in the vehicle in this fog!' Johnston's tone of mild amusement changed as he asked, 'What's the latest on Joe Hawke? Has his wife been informed? Who's minding that side for us?'

'Nothing further. The ACC has asked to be kept in the picture, so the Chief Superintendent is on his way to the hospital. Fiona Hawke has been located and is also on her way. She was collected about half an hour ago. Are you going to deal with Vauxhall? Mind you, there's always the Army.'

'You've got to be joking! We want the job done today! I'll be dealing and I want Wheelbarrow delivered down there, so you'll have to find a driver for that. And check whether the dogs have been called.'

A glance at his watch showed nearly 10.10 so he gave an ETA of 10.25 and set about collecting his papers together ready for the move.

With the knowledge born of long experience, Clem Jones sensed that they were about to move off so, with a quick word of thanks to the small group of policemen to whom he had been talking, he came forward to gather up the gear.

'Vauxhall Cross, on the lamp, suspect car,' said Johnston. Their understanding was now instinctive and made long explanations unnecessary.

Except for a solitary free-lance waiting in the hope of getting a photograph of Andrew Johnston, Liverpool Street Station had returned to normal, as if nothing had happened. The sour smell still persisted, as did the freezing fog, but the travellers, commuters and long-distance alike, were back in the cocoon of their own thoughts and affairs.

Five

The dark blue Hillman, on its way to the Queen Elizabeth Hospital in Woolwich, pulled up at the traffic lights in South Croydon, but Fiona Hawke, sitting silently in the front passenger seat, was completely immersed in her own thoughts. The PC driver, a kindly, experienced man in his mid-forties, respecting her silence, concentrated on his driving. Stationed at Epsom, he was approaching the limits of the area with which he was completely familiar—losing his way at this stage of the trip would not be forgiven and blaming the fog would not be accepted as a valid reason. He had already known before being told to collect Fiona that there had been a serious accident—that sort of news flashes around a police force like a bush fire—and in those circumstances every possible courtesy and attention is given to the next of kin.

Arriving at the house in Chessington he had learned that Fiona Hawke was already on her way to work, and had not received the news; her grown-up son, however, on the point of leaving to catch a train to the West Country, had been able to tell him where she could be found. At the public relations firm where she worked, a short distance away, he had given her the message and then set off with her to Woolwich.

Fiona's thoughts were not quite what one would expect from a wife on such a journey—there were several reasons why—but the sick feeling at the pit of her stomach was entirely normal and could not be dispelled. Not that this was her first experience of the particular form of turmoil, but repetition was not making it any easier to live with.

In her late forties, she had recently celebrated her silver

wedding as the high point of the 'change', a not uncommon experience. Of medium height, inclined to a plumpness which she tried to combat by the careful selection of quality clothes, she was a natural although faded, red-head. She was apprehensive, almost to the point of obsession, about the future and its likely effect on her figure and complexion. She loved her son, Arnold, dearly, and it was a joy when he came back from his work in Bristol to spend the weekend with his parents. On the other hand, seeing him there, now nearly twenty-three, was a constant reminder that she herself was not far off fifty.

The deepening fog was slowing them down, so the driver decided to report progress—or the lack of it—since there appeared to be very little chance of the weather improving. Switching to the message channel he passed a revised ETA to Control and then concentrated yet again on the job in hand, peering past the flicking windscreen wipers into the fog, straining to see any other vehicles early enough to avoid trouble.

His unruffled skill eventually enabled the driver to pull up at the hospital's front entrance at 10.10. Detective Chief Superintendent Bernard Gregory was awaiting their arrival, and, pausing only to thank the driver for his fine effort, he escorted Fiona to the reception area where a tall, distinguished, somewhat formal man, wearing the uniform and insignia of a medical corps lieutenant-colonel, soon appeared and greeted them.

'Good morning, Mrs Hawke. My name is Yates and I am the surgeon in charge. Your husband is in Intensive Care and I need your help with some information about him and his background.' Raising his hand gently to forestall her question, he went on, 'Perhaps it would be better if we went to my office—it's quite near. Let me assure you that this small delay can only serve to help him.'

Recognising the hint, Bernard Gregory stayed where he was, while Colonel Yates led Fiona Hawke away, steering her gently along the corridor while conversing in relaxed tones.

When they reached his office, the orderly calm of which was an outstanding feature even in the context of a large hospital, he settled her deftly and professionally into a comfortable chair. Then, having ascertained her preference, he organised his secretary into producing tea and biscuits, ensuring at the same time that they would not be interrupted.

Yates sat down in the other easy chair at the low table, deliberately well away from the formality of his desk, and reached forward as if to pick up the teapot from the linen-covered tray, but paused to enquire whether she would care to perform the ritual of pouring out. By this simple, well practised, manoeuvre he managed to occupy her in routine domestic activity with the object of relaxing her still further.

'As I mentioned earlier, it would help me if I knew more of your husband's background—perhaps it would be easier if we started by my asking some questions?'

Acquiescing in a low voice, she settled back into her chair.

'Your husband is pretty well developed physically—is he an athletic type?'

'He was, up to a few years ago, but not now. He played a lot of rugby, squash, but his real interest was in athletics, field sports in the main and some weight-lifting. His present job makes it difficult to fit in any sport on a regular basis.'

'Does he drink or smoke heavily?'

Fiona hesitated before replying. How could she admit that with little or no domestic contact between them now, she was not over-familiar with his current habits? Others, she thought, would be more qualified. 'He smokes quite a lot of small cigars, the sort they call manikins, and is a moderate to heavy drinker, but not beer—wine with meals, and whisky.'

'Has he been involved in any accidents before? We've noticed some old scars on his body and legs.'

'Most of those are the results of two rock-climbing accidents that he had some years ago—he had a tendency to over-estimate his ability and take on climbs outside his technical capability or experience. But, what is probably more important from your point of view, he was involved in an earlier explosion in 1976 in Lisburn. There were several pretty serious casualties with Felix in that period. Some were killed.' She paused, then explained, 'Oh, Felix is what the men in the Army and the RUC called all the Ammunition Technical Officers—the bomb disposal officers. Though really their proper military style is either Ammunition Technical Officers or Ammunition Technicians, and Felix is the code-name for the Chief ATO.' She paused again. 'I'm sorry. I'm chattering. You probably know all that anyway.'

Colonel Yates smiled gently. 'Yes, I served in Northern Ireland, Mrs Hawke, and we were all very grateful for what Felix was doing. Perhaps you could give me some more information on that accident? I could, of course, have his army medical record sent here but that would take time.'

'As far as I can remember, a small explosive charge went off in a shop while he was approaching it and he had trouble with his ears. His nose was split open and he had a cut over his left eyebrow. He spent ten days in hospital—I believe they were worried about the possibility of lung damage. I was told that that is a problem quite often in explosions. He has been rather asthmatic since, although it's been difficult to get him to admit it.'

'Thank you very much, Mrs Hawke, you have been most helpful. Now—I've kept you here long enough—perhaps you would like to see your husband.'

Standing beside the bed in the small private room Fiona forced herself to look at her husband as he lay, supine and motionless, on the bed, his face drained of colour, although the blood transfusion bottle to which he was connected was hanging on its frame over the head of the bed. His shallow, barely audible breathing was accompanied by a slight rise and fall of his chest under the sheet and, keeping a firm grip on her emotions, she was aware of a fleeting similarity between the attitude of his upper body and that of a newborn baby. It must be the absence of any pillow under his head, she thought.

The bulge underneath the single sheet showed where the open cage had been positioned over his damaged right leg to protect it from additional knocks while his heavily splinted arm lay motionless by his side, on top of the sheet. The facial cut had obviously not proved to be so serious when cleaned up—its edges were now held together by a series of narrow strips of paper.

Looking down at him, in this room, with its gleaming array of medical equipment and the medical orderly sitting silently, alert and watchful, beside the bed, the strong, antiseptic, rubbery smell mixing with the clinical odour of immaculate sterilised bed linen, she was suddenly aware of the unobtrusive, constant care which was the heart of the medical service's incessant struggle to push back the shadow of death.

Trying to dispel the thought of death, her memory brought back the summer sunshine all those years ago in Hong Kong when she first met Joe. A good-looking, broad-shouldered young sergeant, he had been sitting near her in the Kowloon soft drinks bar, and had started chatting her up in the free and easy style of the colony at his level. The daughter of a senior dockyard official at Taikoo, she knew that there were barriers of rank and social standing between them, but Joe's easy charm did not recognise any distinction. The long contest with her father's bias was finally overcome by the persistence of her nesting instinct; but Joe had to pay the price—an unusual one for him—and consummation was delayed until after the wedding ceremony. But not until after the reception.

Returning from the past with a start, she was aware of an overwhelming desire to throw off the hospital gown and to free herself from the warm, stifling kiss of the medical face-mask. For a brief instant she was ready to flee right out into the fog.

Outside the door she found Colonel Yates and Bernard Gregory sitting in deep conversation, and an orderly came forward to relieve her of the gown and mask. As the two men rose to their feet, she recovered her handbag and, turning to the surgeon, asked, 'What are his chances, please?'

Colonel Yates looked into her face, his regard unwavering and compassionate, sensing the strain and pleading underlying her assumed air of calm, and decided to answer without professional evasion. 'Slightly less than even—but we shan't give in. This is the best-equipped hospital in London and we have a vast fund of experience with these cases.' Seeing her distress, he pressed her to take a seat and asked the Sister to arrange for a cup of tea. He continued, 'Basically, he has a good physique and is a fighter, but the previous explosion is not on his side; neither are the cigars and alcohol. Would you like to stay here? We have the facilities to make you comfortable. I'm bound to say, however, that I don't think your presence will make any difference at this stage.'

The tea arrived and she sat sipping it, the strain on her face slowly easing away. Almost as if to herself she said, 'The fear that they all live with is of ending up like a cabbage. They accept the possibility of death—it's the devil that they fight every time, and they're confident in their ability to stay alive. But, if it all goes wrong, to be totally dependent on others for their very existence . . .' Making an obvious effort, she brought the two men back into focus. 'Thank you, no. I shan't stay. You need the rooms for people who have to come a long way. I've got to tell my son, and I must keep myself occupied.'

Bernard Gregory broke in, 'The car is still outside and I've arranged for a WPC to be with you. I've made my report to the ACC, and whatever you need you know you've only got to ask.' Turning to the surgeon, he said, 'That telephone number that I gave you is manned day and night and I think it would be best if you use us as the message centre. We'll do anything that you ask. Policemen think a lot of these chaps.'

At the front door of the hospital, Fiona Hawke and Bernard Gregory made their farewells to the tall military figure and then moved off into the fog, on their way back to the car park. Joe's wife was starting to droop; she was losing her sparkle—the long sickening wait had started. If he survived, however, Joe Hawke had probably saved his marriage, though he would not have chosen to do so in that way.

Bernard Gregory was making his way back to the reception area and a telephone when, through the swirling fog, he saw a police Range Rover standing at the other end of the car park. He realised that it was Joe Hawke's vehicle and, reaching it, he opened the door to find the driver sitting there keeping vigil in the warm while listening to the traffic on the Force radio. After Joe had been admitted, his enquiries about the Explosives Officer's condition, predictably, had produced little information—it was far too soon—so he decided to wait it out for a time in the car park. The Chief Superintendent now saw the Range Rover as an opportunity too good to be missed so, after stopping at the main entrance to make his telephone call, he used it to get back to the Yard where, summoned to the ACC, he reported on Joe's condition.

Her elderly aunt's voice carried down the stairs. 'Jean! Switch on Radio Four quickly—there's an important news flash.'

Jean Johnston leaned across the table in the breakfast room and switched channels.

. . . ails are not available. A further report has been received that the Central Line section of Liverpool Street station has been closed since eight o'clock this morning. No information is available on the emergency, which has seriously delayed many City commuters, but it is thought to involve another bomb threat. We will bring you more news as it comes in. And now back to the studio . . .

Going through to the kitchen she finished making the mid-morning cup of tea, poured out two cups and carried them upstairs to the old lady's room.

'Did you hear the news flash?' her aunt asked.

'Not the start of it, but I heard about Liverpool Street. I wonder if Andy is there—he's on this morning.'

'Yes, I heard the Range Rover leave before I went to the

bathroom. The first part was about an explosion at Greenwich and said that a police explosive expert is in hospital.'

Jean's heart lurched and she asked, 'Did they say what time it happened? Did they give any name?'

'No. That's all they said. Do you think it's him?'

'I'm sure that the office would have been on to let me know if it was.' She did not sound wholly confident but had been part of the scene for a very long time and had learned the value of patience.

'Why don't you ring them up and find out?'

'Oh, no. They'll be busy enough without me. I've never been one for that. Anyway, one of the wives used to be ringing up all the time and Andy got very irritated about it! He's always kept his family life and his official life apart from each other.'

When they had finished, she picked up the tray with the dirty crockery on it, went back downstairs, and washed up, then slowly dried up and put the clean items away. She switched off the radio, glanced out of the breakfast room window, looking down at the washing hanging, stiff as boards and unmoving, on the rotary clothes line in the fog, then decided to return upstairs for company. Routine activities could only be sustained for so long.

Jean Johnston had been conscripted into the ATS in late 1943 and had served in the orderly room of a mixed anti-aircraft battery, the Army making use of her civilian skills in shorthand and typing. By 1943 the military hierarchy were coming round to a radical new policy of checking on people's abilities before assigning them to duty. There was still a volume of opinion, however, that this type of thinking would put the Army back at least a decade—how else were they going to keep the instructors in the UK away from all that unpleasantness overseas, except by training drivers to be cooks, cooks to be clerks, clerks to be riflemen and, every once in a while, sending a job lot off for officer training?

Andy had been in the Army too, and after the war, their respective postings branches contrived, unknowingly, to place them together in a decaying hutted camp, starting a sequence that culminated in a post-commissioning military wedding, and so Private Jean Warley, translated to civilian life by the process of demobilisation with her age and service group, once more entered into the military atmosphere, now in a supportive role. Sixteen years of army marriage, with fourteen different homes, had produced two daughters and two sons, each, not surprisingly in the circumstances, born in a different town.

Truly married, from the start, into the enclosed world of the explosives specialist, she had become accustomed to its demands, dangers and irregular routine, drawing great solace from the role of mothering her family at home and overseas, in private and official accommodation, mostly in that precarious state of financial balance that British governments considered appropriate to their professional, peacetime regular forces. Kipling had said it all before and was ignored for his pains!

Her deep-rooted yearning for stability and 'a house of her own' was now satisfied at long last, but the unpredictable nature of her husband's work was still an unsettling, nagging presence. Still, like so many others in her position, she maintained a diplomatic silence. Her daughters now flown into their own domestic circles, she was, nevertheless, providing every home comfort and service to Andy and two tall adult sons and the elderly aunt.

The sight of the old lady immersed in her knitting struck a responsive chord and, having dug out a half-finished pullover from some obscure hiding place, she settled down in an atmosphere of mutual support. This calming partnership, sustained by reminiscing conversation, continued until the radio news at ten o'clock which, although a little more detailed, added very little to what they had heard earlier.

Six

Coyle and Walsh had made it back to base—a classically uneventful retreat from contact, providing mutual cover for each other without attracting attention. With Walsh, the Londoner, leading the way, they joined the Piccadilly Line and then on to Holloway Road Underground station from where, through the freezing fog, they moved carefully along seedy, deteriorating side roads to Martineau Road in the Drayton Park area. Their 'safe house', similar in character to the one that Brendan O'Loughlin occupied in Highbury Park, was a cheap conversion by a speculative landlord, sparsely furnished. It had four storeys and thus four flats. Like all terrorists, Coyle and Walsh had chosen the top flat. Its rudimentary facilities and relatively low rent suited the IRA with its need for cash-spending anonymity.

Sleep was the dominant thought in their minds and, having completed the basic security checks, they zipped themselves up into individual sleeping bags laid out on the double bed and in a few minutes were dead to the world.

Janice Leroy had been shopping in Essex Road and around the Islington Green area, an expedition involving great concentration on prices and bargain offers. Even so, the shopping bag suspended from one handle of the twin-seat, fold-up push-chair was still only half full—housekeeping money seemed to stretch less with every week that passed. A bottle-assisted blonde, her last hair-do now beyond easy recall, the spiky straggling hair framed a plain, care-worn face, much older than its true age of twenty-five. With brown eyes set in a pale, almost pasty complexion, she wore no make-up and her full-breasted, thickening figure was protected against the cold only by a shabby, thin tweed coat.

Now that the money in her purse had almost gone, she pushed the twin-seater away from Essex Road and down Pakington Street towards the rather dilapidated older-type council flat where she lived as Washington Leroy's common-law wife. A three-year-old boy and an eighteen-month-old girl, the two children in the push chair were obviously the products of a union of white woman and black man.

Arriving at the entrance to the block of flats, tired and dispirited, Janice backed up the step and pulled the two-seater with its sleepy load to the floor level in the entrance hall. Preoccupied with completing the manoeuvre without waking her children she failed to hear the slight sound of movement behind her as the dishevelled figure of a man left the cover of the space under the stone stairs. The thrust of a hard object into her side brought a shriek of pained surprise which was cut short by a hoarse whisper. 'Keep quiet, you stupid English bitch, and do as you're bloody well told. Which is your flat?'

In a quavering voice she replied, 'Number nineteen, on the first floor. What do you want to know for?'

'That's where we're going, and keep your trap shut, you stupid bloody woman. Come on, lift this damned contraption.'

Seizing one end of the two-seater and becoming even more frenetically enraged at her lack of instant co-operation, he thrust her savagely back towards the stairs and then, backwards, up them. Her eyes fixed on him in terror, she stumbled several times, adding to his impatience.

Quietly, without his noticing, the door to one of the ground-floor flats opened about two inches and an elderly male eye peered out. Glimpsing the automatic thrusting towards the terrified woman, the eye's owner, the caretaker, quietly closed the door and retreated into his flat.

The two children, now awake and screaming, added to the clamour echoing up the bare walls of the stairwell as the gunman forced his way up to the first floor and across the landing towards the door of No. 19. Shaking with fear and almost dropping her purse, Janice, her mind benumbed by the cries of her children, fished out the door key and forced it into the lock with trembling fingers.

As the noise of the slamming door reverberated up and down the stairs, cutting off the cries, the caretaker picked up his telephone and dialled 999.

Sean McAllister had surfaced, armed and vicious, and was now located—in police parlance, 'housed'. Time: 10.15.

As Andrew Johnston opened the door of the Range Rover he said, without preamble, 'What do you think, then?'

Clem Jones, who had been warming up the engine, looked across at him. 'Eh? What about?' There were times when you needed a crystal ball degree to keep up with the man—he did it deliberately.

'The weather. The road conditions. You're the bloody driver—what the hell did you think I was asking about? Some bit of crumpet that you've had your eye on?'

Clem grinned. 'I might have known you wouldn't be asking about anything interesting. Road conditions? Well, we won't be able to make maximum. As well as the fog and ice there's always the great British motorist—you can bet on him being a right pain in the arse!'

'Not to a Class One, surely? Not to one of Hendon's finest!'

While this well-rehearsed banter was going on, Bomb Two had moved away from the station, down Old Broad Street, and was turning into London Wall. Andrew went on the air and confirmed the ETA; the situation at Vauxhall remained unaltered, said Control.

With a final word to Ethel, confirming the Isle of Dogs pick-up point, Nicos Georgiou pushed off, got the outboard started and turned the elderly rubber dinghy downstream with his back to Chiswick Bridge, its stone spans barely visible through the fog which muffled the sounds from traffic crawling across it. Ethel, his wife, stood by the gravel patch until the craft and its crew disappeared from sight, then, as the sound of the outboard was swallowed up by the fog, climbed back into the car and drove apprehensively away. It was only after fifty yards that she remembered to switch on the lights. Time: 10.30.

Nicos, brought to England at the age of fifteen by his Greek-Cypriot parents was a kitchen hand-cum-waiter in a small local restaurant, struggling to keep himself and his family above the poverty line. To bolster the family finances, Ethel, a native of Battersea, went out to work as a cleaner in a local bank.

Their children, John, aged fourteen, and Carlo, ten and a half, were on a short half-term holiday from their comprehensive and both parents had managed to wangle the day off to give the boys the treat of a boat trip from Mortlake to the Isle of Dogs, not on a Thames pleasure boat but in the family craft.

A short, dishevelled, swarthy figure, still half-asleep and scratching his chest, Nicos had been draining his second cup of coffee earlier that morning when the hurricane struck. The thunder of two pairs of feet on the stairs competed with shrill voices raised in disagreement, voices with Mediterranean intensity and a fervid belief in the sheer joy of sustained argument. Bursting noisily in through the kitchen doorway, they were silenced immediately by a sharp word from their mother. Nicos never had the same effect on them—the love of argument as an art form came from him, after all. Ethel, a faded blonde wearing a wrap-round pinafore, had already cooked his breakfast and was seated at the kitchen table in no mood to put up with noisy kids.

The two boys, each attacking a bowl of cereals, fell to discussing the forthcoming trip enthusiastically, referring every point to their father for adjudication then, like chattering starlings, immediately challenging the answers.

Once he had finished his breakfast, Nicos went to the back door and, intent on perpetuating the maritime image, stepped outside to sniff the weather. Scantily clad as he was, the fog and frost hit him with shattering force and his nautical enthusiasm slumped with the speed of a candled parachute.

Turning around, he saw John and Carlo standing in the doorway, their eager faces tinged with apprehension as they sensed his unfavourable reaction to the weather. Wordlessly, he pushed them inside and closed the door, while Ethel, now at the sink, gave all her attention to the washing up in a positive act of withdrawal from the discussion.

Predictably, it was Carlo who spoke first—he was at the age where eagerness and childish anticipation were not compromised by the ability to judge atmosphere, to know and recognise the advantages of expediency. 'Papa, what time are we leaving? How long will it take?'

Ethel and John froze, holding their breath, and waited for the reply.

'I don't think we should go,' said Nicos. 'It's a long way to the Isle of Dogs and the weather is not good. The boat is not strong, it is cold and there is fog.'

'But, Dad, you promised,' wailed John. 'We've been looking forward to this since Christmas—we've been working on it. The other boys at school know all about it, and if we don't go they will take the mickey.'

Rising to the challenge, to the offer of discussion, Nicos argued volubly against going, his fear of the project coming close to the surface, until his wife, tired and with her nerves in shreds, broke in. 'For God's sake, Nick, take them, you've been going on about the trip for weeks. And I'm looking forward to a day to myself.'

As they got clothes together and assembled provisions for the trip the smiles on the boys' faces were almost bright enough to drive the fog back across the river. Already, mentally, they were part of the next Arctic expedition. Nicos was less confident.

Ethel, pressed into service as chauffeuse, was worried by

the fog lurking close to the surface of the river. As it was, the car came unexpectedly on the narrow tarmac of Thames Bank, and making a late, frantic effort to apply the worn brakes, she only just managed to stop it in time. The family transport was a rusting, scabrous, once green Standard Vanguard, a mouldering question mark against the MOT system. Its strongest part was the roof rack. Flustered, Ethel noisily and jerkily reversed the car to the top of the gravel patch, where Nicos and the boys unroped the inflatable to slide it off the roof rack. Not quite fully inflated, the eight-foot craft was difficult to handle, bending suddenly to drag its centre on the gravel but, to the inevitable accompaniment of noisy disagreements, they finally got it afloat at the tiny, green-painted pier at the rear of the old warehouse-style building, famous worldwide as Watney's Mortlake Brewery, and shipped the outboard.

Whenever he was driving through London, memories of past 'incidents' flooded into Andrew Johnston's mind as he passed the sites where they had occurred. Clem Jones swung the Range Rover into Old Bailey and past the entrance to the Central Criminal Court, and Johnston saw again in vivid detail the scene which had met his eyes in 1973 when the whole area had been devastated by a car bomb. The glass tower block of offices with every window shattered, back and front . . . the fractured water main flooding the road . . . the wrecked pub . . . the police traffic car definitely past its best . . . the pigeons, grounded featherless, with their de-flèched quills making them look like grotesque, mis-shapen grey hedgehogs, huddled against the foot of the solid granite walls, alive, shivering but totally in shock . . . If anybody wanted a demonstration of the differing effects of large explosive charges on traditionally solid buildings and modern glass monstrosities that was where he should have been.

As Bomb Two approached the river, the fog grew thicker and they were forced to crawl across Ludgate Circus where several City policemen were doing their determined best to prevent those drivers who were still mobile from committing suicide.

The time for decision had arrived, so Andrew Johnston said, 'Right at Blackfriars and along the Embankment. I don't fancy the other side of the river in this lot.'

Swinging left across Westminster Bridge for the second time that day, they heard Big Ben's half-chimes announce half-past ten, but by then they were on the other side of the river, rounding the roundabout, turning into Lambeth Palace Road and speeding on past the fire brigade headquarters towards Vauxhall. They were halted by a line of flashing blue lights stretching across the road at Tinworth Street, a quarter of a mile or so from Vauxhall Cross, where the suspect car had been reported.

A Metropolitan Police sergeant walked towards them and, recognising Andrew Johnston, told him, 'The Control Point is in Pendennis House and MP Mobile is in position around the back. You've been pretty busy today, Major—it's a good job that we've got you chaps.'

Bomb Two drew up beside the mobile control van. Getting out, Andrew poked his head into the warm, cramped space: 'Will you show Bomb Two arriving at 10.35?' Ten minutes late, but in the circumstances it was a bloody miracle. Clem Jones had worked his usual wonders.

Stepping into the van, he saw that one of the occupants was an inspector, who was sitting in front of a large-scale plan of the area.

'Who's about?' asked Andrew; turning his head, the inspector replied, 'Not as many as you'd think! Most of them are staying in the warm waiting for your confirmation—or otherwise. The district commander is on the scene, Trafpol have got a chief superintendent here, the navy's afloat and the Press Bureau's man is performing—sod his luck, he's going to have a job if you say the thing's for real! Your office would like you to ring them.'

* * *

The shrill clamour of the telephone bell splitting the silence seemed to fill the whole house, even penetrating the old lady's variable deafness, and brought them both up short, the atmosphere electric.

Jean went into the next room, picked up the handset and, heart in mouth, pressed it to her ear.

'Mrs Johnston?'

'Yes.'

'Detective-Sergeant Brockway, from the office. Have you been listening to the radio?'

'Oh, yes.' (*Why doesn't he get on with it?*)

'Well, the situation is this. Joe Hawke was pretty badly hurt at Greenwich and his wife has been taken to see him. Andy has been to the scene but was called away to deal with a problem at Liverpool Street. That turned out to be a hoax.'

'Oh! Thanks for ringing up to tell me. I wondered if he was involved. He seems to have been pretty busy. Is Mrs Hawke all right? Does she need any help?'

'Not so far as I know—that is being covered by the Yard at the moment. But your husband is still involved, I'm afraid. There's a bit of bother at Vauxhall, although we are not fully in the picture so I can't say whether it's a live one or not. It seems likely to drag on a bit but as soon as we can we'll let you know what's happening.'

'Thank you very much for phoning, Nigel. Don't feel that you have to do it too often, but I would appreciate the occasional message. Andy won't ring, that's sure.'

Replacing the handset, she returned to the old lady's room where they fell to discussing the news animatedly. After a few minutes, Jean suggested making some more tea, and going down to the kitchen, she busied herself with the kettle and setting out the crockery, deliberately switching on her domestic thoughts to exclude the others. Then, she set her mind to solving one of the recurring problems of her life—what to get for lunch.

Seven

Nigel Brockway answered when Andrew dialled the office number. 'I thought you'd better know—we've been swamped with calls from duty officers with problems, at least they think they're problems. I've got about sixteen stacked up, some through the post—they can wait—and some carrier bags. We can't put those off so I'm getting Don Reynolds and Frank Norrie to come in a bit early. Did the Wheelbarrow get there OK?'

'I've only just arrived so I haven't checked on Wheelbarrow yet. I haven't been to the scene yet or seen anybody dealing with it. If it's a runner, I reckon that it'll be some time with this fog. Is there any more news of Joe?'

Nigel brought him up to date on Joe Hawke's condition but had to ring off because one of the other telephones was demanding his attention. It looked as if he was going to be rather more heavily engaged on the Commissioner's business than normal.

Turning back to the Control Point inspector, Andrew established that the Wheelbarrow van was parked at the side of Pendennis House, but the driver who had delivered it had returned to duty north of the river. The plan of the Vauxhall Cross area was subjected to detailed scrutiny and then, after a short but useful discussion, he made to leave but, pausing at the door, asked for details of the communications set-up covering the scene.

'We're operating here on Force radio but all other Force sets in the area are switched off. The local link is being maintained on personal radio—it's lower-powered, you know, and nobody is nearer to the car than thirty-five yards. The River boats are on Force radio.'

Nodding his thanks, Andrew Johnston left the van, climbed into the Range Rover, and Clem Jones, driving out on to Albert Embankment, turned left away from the bridge, right at The Crown, under a railway bridge and into a succession of back streets, and so to one end of a wide pedestrian tunnel.

After leaving the pier, Nicos had settled in the stern, hunched against the cold, with his hand on the combined throttle and tiller arm of the motor, his face already showing the strain of concentration. The two boys had taken up positions forward, huddled together and facing their father, getting some shelter from the small yellow canvas dodger fixed to the craft's bow, any apprehension that they might be feeling about the boat's movement still subordinated to the tremendous excitement that had been building up in them for days.

As the grey-painted steelwork of Barnes railway bridge loomed over them, further increasing bad visibility, they were making poor progress on top of the tide with only limited power coming from the elderly engine. Less than perfectly inflated, the craft sat low in the water, increasing the demand on the engine and raising the fuel consumption.

With the noise of the slamming door still reverberating around the flat, McAllister shoved the protesting woman and the loaded two-seater straight across the small hallway and through the half-opened door opposite.

With the two children now terrified, screaming and sobbing alternately, their mother reacted like a cornered lioness angrily protecting her cubs. Her face flushed and her eyes darkening with hate, she took an angry step towards the gunman. 'Who do you think you are, pushing people about? There's nothing here worth taking, so you might as well bugger off while there's still time!' Stooping, she started to comfort her children while releasing the straps that held them in. In her present mood of outraged motherhood she was totally oblivious of the rising danger that the noise and tension were creating.

McAllister, rapidly losing what little self-control was normally part of his make-up, was teetering on the edge of certifiability. Smashing the barrel of his automatic down on her back, his features contorted with anger, he hissed, 'Shut your face, you English bitch, or I'll do for you and your two black bastards. Where's the telephone?'

Sobbing now, the pain from the blow flooding her crumpled body, Janice was coming to realise that blind opposition was not going to help—only by going along with his demands could she hope to protect her children and herself. Recovering her feet and continuing to unbuckle the straps, she told him that there was no phone in the flat. No one in the block had one, except for the caretaker downstairs.

The news hit him like a blow from a sledgehammer. In McAllister's childlike reasoning there had to be a telephone just because he had assumed that it would be so. How else could he deal with the authorities? Watching him with horrified fascination, Janice could see him straining for an answer—a follower used to receiving orders trying desperately to assume the role of clear-thinking leader. In his frustration he aimed a violent kick at the two-seater, fortunately now empty, and projected it forcibly across the room to crash into the fireplace, shattering the glowing ash into the hearth.

The room in which the gunman now found himself was the living room with its window looking out on to the main street. Furnished with a few sticks gathered painfully together from jumble sales and junk shops it seemed suddenly to press in on him. Twitching with nerves, he took off on a journey of exploration, pushing Janice before him. The short tour disclosed a kitchen, two bedrooms, a bathroom/toilet and no way out except the front door. Even to his suspicious, red-rimmed eyes there was no sign of a telephone. They went back to the living room.

Despite the meagreness of her larder stock, the habit of

years asserted itself and Janice decided to make a drink for herself and the children. That's if he'll let me, she thought. Perhaps he's thirsty too! It might help to calm him down a bit.

She asked him if he would like a cup of tea.

'Sod off, you stupid bitch! Haven't you got anything stronger? Tea-drinking's for women and ministers!'

Remembering that there were some bits and pieces left over from a party, she went across to the battered sideboard and, raking around inside, produced about a third of a bottle of rum, together with a small amount of Southern Comfort. Snatching them from her, he found a glass tumbler and, returning to the front room, poured in all the whisky, which he drank in one convulsive gulp.

All this time, the two children had been cowering in a sagging rexine-covered easy chair, wide-eyed and whimpering with fear. When McAllister waved her into the kitchen, she made to take them with her. His reaction was instantaneous. Shouting at her to stop, he told her that the boy had to stay and that if she did anything stupid she knew what would happen. Stilling her desperate protests by the simple expedient of pointing his automatic at her son, McAllister finally agreed that she could take the children, in turn, to the toilet but was adamant that the boy must stay with him while she made the tea.

Listening to the sounds from the kitchen as he attacked the remainder of the rum, he became increasingly aware of the noise of unusual activity coming from the street outside. Lurching to his feet, with his gun in his hand, he staggered across to the window to stare out. The local police were engaged in evacuation and setting up a cordon.

Rushing into the kitchen, he grabbed Janice Leroy by the arm and dragged her to the window, the lower half of which he threw up with a crash. Forcing her to stand in front of the opening so that he was concealed from view, he screamed down at the police, 'Hey you, this is the Provos, you bloody Sassenachs. If you think you can get me out of here just try it.

I'll shoot the bloody lot of you, and this bitch and her bloody kids will get it as well!'

He twisted her arm savagely to make her speak. Crying again, she called out, 'He's telling the truth and he's got a gun. My two babies are here and he's going to kill them!'

The window slammed shut as she was dragged back into the room.

The roadway emerging from the west end of Vauxhall Bridge ran straight across the embankment and, passing under the complex of railway lines, became Kennington Lane. On the other side of the railway, Kennington Lane occupied itself with reaching Newington while Lambeth Road, aiming at Stockwell, swung away to the right and, between them, the one-way route from the Oval fed in via Harleyford Road. Two pedestrian tunnels, one on each side of Kennington Lane, pierced the embankment under the railway lines and, when Bomb Two drew up near the entrance of the westernmost one, Andrew Johnston saw a small group standing just within its shelter.

One personality dominated the group—Chief Superintendent Herbert Smith—the governor of Kennington Lane Police Station, its boss, the Führer. His statutory thirty years now well past, he was an old-time policeman, experienced, rather overweight, barrel-chested, with war ribbons up, exuding an air of total, practical competence. Always at the front of any operation, he led by example, with the ability to strip any situation of its irrelevancies, and possessed the hearts and minds of all of his men—a rare accomplishment, growing rarer.

He was talking to Peter Barwell, the duty officer who had been at the scene from the start. A late entrant into police service, Inspector Barwell had served in Northern Ireland as a corporal in the Parachute Regiment and it showed in his carriage and air of controlled confidence. His neatly barbered red hair was complemented by a neatly trimmed moustache, and his raincoat and uniform, even at this stage of his tour of duty, were immaculate. Another natural leader with an instinct for the proper line of action, he was a perfect foil for Bert Smith. The Chief Superintendent motioned him forward, introducing him to Andrew Johnston and recommending him as the best person to provide a run-down on the situation.

'We received a Telex from Control at 09.03 about a suspect car under the railway at Vauxhall. There had been a coded call and we were told to look at it urgently. The car was reported as a grey and green Consort but no other details were given. The caller did not give a time but said the bomb would go off if we tried to move the car.'

Bert Smith proffered a piece of paper. 'I've got a copy of the message here but it doesn't tell us anything else.'

Peter Barwell resumed, 'I came down here and had a quick look around the area and found this car. It's a grey and green Consort, index UWC 368F, and when we put it up it came back stolen from Hemel Hempstead three days ago. I had a quick look through the window—there's a small cardboard box on the rear seat. So we called you.'

As he reached into his trouser pocket for a handkerchief, his unbuttoned raincoat swung back to give a glimpse of two medal ribbons—the Military Medal and the Campaign Service Medal with the oak-leaf emblem on it. He added, 'I was in the Paras in Londonderry, 1972, so I didn't hang about near the car. We started clearing the area straight away but I needed more men.'

'Just where is the car?' asked Johnston.

'In Lambeth Place, under the middle of the bridge, opposite the bus stop. There are still two buses there. I don't think the drivers are particularly enthusiastic about moving them.'

'Thanks very much, Mr Barwell. It's such a help when a scene starts off on the right foot—or perhaps I should say the *left* foot, with a full pace of thirty inches to follow! I congratulate you and I'm very grateful. There's no doubt that your Northern Ireland experience helped.'

Turning to Bert Smith, he asked, 'Can you fill me in on the current situation? I've got to decide where I shall work from.'

'The cordon is established along South Lambeth Road, Parry Street, Wandsworth Road, across Bridgefoot and into Kennington Road. That's the inner cordon, but traffic is also being blocked off at suitable places three to four hundred yards away and nothing is being allowed on to Vauxhall Bridge. River Division has a stop boat about a quarter of a mile upstream and one at Westminster Bridge—the fog isn't helping them! The railway people have stopped all trains past Queens Road and nothing is leaving Waterloo main-line station at all. That's about the lot. Oh, yes—the Underground! The Jubilee Line from Brixton is still running through in both directions but we can stop it if you want.'

Andrew Johnston, who knew the area pretty well—it was on one of his normal routes—was quite satisfied with the arrangements. Bert Smith's grasp of the traffic arrangements was masterly but quite typical. He said, 'I'm going to have a further look around, Bert. If the car proves to be positive I shall want to see a number of people—railway, bus, Underground, gas, electricity, water—you know the sort of thing I'm sure.'

As Andrew walked back out of the tunnel towards his vehicle, accompanied by Peter Barwell, a thought struck him and, pointing to another entrance further along, he queried, 'Isn't that the entrance to Vauxhall Station?'

The station proper was above their heads and extended from the other side of Kennington Road, almost as far as Lambeth Place, with eight platforms, each over one hundred yards long. The four lines passing through this station carried every part of the rail traffic entering or leaving Waterloo main-line station.

'Yes, it goes right the way through to the other side. The ticket office is at the other end and it's the only way up to the station, although there is another way down on the side facing the bridge. All the railway staff have been pulled out and I've got a PC in there in case somebody gets through.'

'Good. I wonder if you could do me a favour? Could you get on to MP Mobile and get them to send my Wheelbarrow van forward to here? The keys should be in the ignition. Could you also ask them to get in touch with my office. I'd like Len Pound to come down here—it looks as if I'll be able to use him. Tell him to bring a bomb jacket and helmet. I'd call him myself, but I don't want to use the Force radio and I'm not on your net. Thanks, Peter.'

It would be some time before Wheelbarrow arrived and, feeling the itch to get on with the job, he decided to get a better view of the car. If you didn't watch it these jobs could drag on and, before you knew it, you could lose another hour.

Using a roundabout route Clem Jones drove the Range Rover to the corner of Langley Lane, opposite the end of Lambeth Place. A quick survey showed that there was no chance of a direct line of sight from the pavement—the railings in the centre of the road were in the way—so he got Clem to manoeuvre the vehicle into position with its bonnet pointing away from the car with just one rear corner peering around the edge of the Interplanetary Society's building.

Setting up the spotter 'scope on the vehicle roof he stretched out behind it with the high-intensity lamp at his side. Settling himself as comfortably as he could he made a deliberate study of the tunnel, ignoring the intense cold as he peered through the fog. He saw a grimy, shadowy area of broken, filthy pavements enclosed by the steel girders of the railway bridge supported on tall, dirt-encrusted brick walls. The girders, scabbed with rust, their rivets standing out like regimented goosepimples, rested at an angle across the walls and served as a roosting, courting and breeding pitch for squadrons of pigeons. They had done for years if the accumulated evidence was any guide.

Two red double-decker buses stood, unlit and abandoned, against the left-hand kerb, near the other end of the tunnel, mutely celebrating their success in reaching the destination after fighting through the fog from Wallington and Mitcham. Nearer, on the opposite side of the road—for road it was: the main road across the river from Stockwell—stood the suspect. A battered Ford Consort, colour and index indistinguishable in the weak light from the overhead strip lamps, it was parked partly on the pavement, angled with its rear bumper touching the wall and its bonnet pointing away from him.

Filthy, crumpled paper, beer cans, empty cigarette packets, discarded bottles, obstructed the gutters and littered the pavements, sometimes lying in pools of water at the base of the glistening moisture-streaks running down the walls. He had worked in more attractive areas, but sites for terrorist bombs were not selected to advance the cause of tourism. In any case, a scene would have to be particularly revolting to intrude at all into the concentration, the total application that was part of his work.

Directing the beam of light from his lamp across the road on to the car helped with two problems: it indicated that it probably wasn't a light-sensitive device, and the colours and index number of the vehicle were confirmed. It was also unusual and interesting to see the light beam clearly defined in its path through the fog like a solid gleaming bar rigidly fixed to the front of the lamp.

Away to the right, the noise of a door slamming shut told him that Wheelbarrow's Transit van had arrived, so Johnston slid off the roof and, repacking the 'scope and lamp, they made their way back to the rendezvous.

Seeing Peter Barwell again, he took the opportunity to deal with some problems that had been worrying him. 'Peter, the pub at the other end of Lambeth Place. I could see lights shining out—has it been evacuated? And what about the houses at the end of Vauxhall Grove and Langley Lane? They're in direct line.'

'The pub—it's The Elephant and Castle—was evacuated earlier but the lights weren't on then. I'll get one of the chaps to check it. Langley Lane and Vauxhall Grove have been evacuated.'

'When you look through the tunnel towards the river there's a very high building across Bridgefoot, a building nearly twenty storeys high, full of windows. It's in direct line with the car, about a hundred and fifty yards away. If that car goes, if it is a bomb, that building will be a slaughter house.'

'That's Camelford House and it's the Regional Headquarters of the Telecommunications Region, so there's likely to be some attempt to keep some staff in there. And Pendennis House is right behind it, of course!'

'Well, I appreciate that some buildings have to be treated differently but I think that it should definitely be evacuated. Do you think that your commander could deal with it? He's down that end now and he's certainly got the clout.'

'OK. I'll contact MP Mobile and ask him to do it.'

Having left the railway bridge behind, with the inflatable holding the centre of the river, Nicos found difficulty in making out the details of each bank. There was little enough to see on the left bank in any case with its expanse of playing fields but, on the opposite bank, the river wall, backed with houses, made position-keeping easier. This navigational aid disappeared quite quickly, however, with the houses retreating from the winding river and the wall giving way to trees, their branches trailing in the water to trap unsightly floating debris.

With the cold damp silence of the river scene broken only by the thin beat of the engine, John reached for the plastic grip standing on the bottom board near his feet: excitement having abated slightly and with nothing to distract him, another youthful craving was taking over—he was hungry! Quickly unzipping the bag he took out a paper-wrapped package.

Like all wives and mothers, Ethel had assembled sufficient provisions for an army—an expression of the nervous tension and concern building up before the fledgelings escaped from her influence. Sandwiches, fruit cake, an apple and a KitKat each and a flask of tea—the English influence outweighing the expected Cypriot cuisine.

Ever alert to any possibility of a snack, Carlo's appetite was aroused instantly. He asked hopefully, 'What have we got? What's in the sandwiches? Can we start on them, Papa? Oh, please, Papa!'

Nicos, now fully occupied in varying the line which the inflatable had been following, uttered a perfunctory affirmative and turned back to his own problem. With Chiswick Eyot looming up ahead he had failed to appreciate that the river was curving towards the right and he could now see two channels, the narrower left-hand one quite clearly defined, but the other, much wider, less clear. His right arm, already cold and cramped, was unconsciously taking the craft towards the narrow channel against the Chiswick bank.

The excited movements of his two sons disturbed the craft's rather uncertain trim and caused it to rock fairly violently, producing, in him, a tiny flutter of doubt. Jeans, shirt, pullover and anorak were scarcely adequate in this combination of fog and frost, particularly when blood-warming exercise was denied, and his failure to dress properly against this weather was already having an effect, slowing his reactions.

Uttering a sharp word of reprimand to John, he switched his attention back to the route ahead and decided, by a simple process of unplanned reflex action, to take the right-hand channel. Forced into recognising that the river did not run a straight course but meandered along in a series of serpentine bends, Nicos, now also munching sandwiches, settled down to steer a better line.

After a while he saw an Emmettesque structure creeping out of the fog around the river bend ahead. A tracery of buff and white painted metal suspended from two highly decorative towers topped by fairy pinnacles, the road line of Hammersmith Bridge was marked by a broad band of latticed girders. As the inflatable moved onwards between the massive stone piers it was possible to discern that each crossing point of the latticework was embellished somewhat incongruously with a golden star. The day was certainly not golden and stars there were not.

* * *

Wheelbarrow is a small remote-handling vehicle, three and a half feet long, shaped like a tank. It has two independently controlled rubber caterpillar tracks and is steered using a closed-circuit TV camera which sends back a picture to a monitor screen. Mounted on top of the 'tank' is an adjustable boom capable of movement upwards, downwards, forwards and backwards, using two electric motors. Most of the ancillary equipment, such as a multi-shot shotgun, lifting or window-breaking gear, is mounted on this boom, as is a powerful lamp.

Manoeuvring Wheelbarrow by means of a hand-held control box connected to the vehicle by a multi-core cable which trails out as it moves, the expert operator can examine, dismantle or destroy suspect explosive devices, lift them to alternative locations, cut wiring, take X-rays, place explosive or incendiary charges, facilitate the movement of small cars, open doors, climb stairs—all from distances of up to one hundred metres.

Designed to avoid the temptation to the bomb disposal officer to approach the suspect device or vehicle unnecessarily, or stay in the danger area too long, Wheelbarrow has been used under widely differing conditions and in many countries, being regarded as infinitely more disposable than human beings.

Andrew Johnston was pleased to see that an available Wheelbarrow had been run down its ramp from the Transit and was now parked close to the wall, ten yards short of Lambeth Place. Len Pound, the technician, had come down from Whitehall in a wireless car and was engaged in carrying out the final adjustments, marking up the screen of the TV monitor with the signs essential to successful control of the equipment. This finished, he fitted the long cable, checked that the shotgun was fully loaded and carried out the final test of all functions, pressing the buttons and switches on the control unit in turn.

Minutes later, Clem Jones was sitting in the Transit, studying the picture on the TV monitor as he steered

Wheelbarrow forward while Len Pound carefully paid out the essential, delicate, multi-core cable, concentrating on protecting its steadily unrolling length from damage. The semi-darkness in the back of the van enabled Clem to study the TV monitor more easily while operating the controls and switches on the hand-held unit. Both men were experts. They had to be—any damage to the cable, any other serious failure, could convert this life-protecting, all-purpose equipment into a frustrated, impotent lump of expensive junk, a piece of petrified, grotesque technology or a madly gyrating, demonic runaway.

A staggeringly large total of hours of tense, challenging, difficult operational experience in all weathers, mostly in Northern Ireland, by countless exponents, some at virtuoso level, at times under sniper-fire, had developed techniques whose detailed, reliable routines were practised wherever Wheelbarrow was used.

Crouching beside Clem Jones, Andrew Johnston indicated that he wanted the tracked vehicle to move out into the road and then take a wide swing to the right in order to provide an operating reserve of cable, sufficient to avoid strain on plugs and drive-motors. The viewers saw it lurch down into the gutter, pause as if to summon its reserves of energy and then, its ridged rubber tracks grasping the road surface with grim determination, move inexorably but obliquely up the road camber to a point near the road island at the tunnel threshold.

The spotlights,—whose axes were synchronised with the TV camera and the weapon boom—now switched on, the vehicle was manoeuvred carefully but firmly into position at the top of the camber in the tunnel. While turning on to the approach axis, a fleeting hazy picture of two buses flashed into view, at the extreme edge of vision, on the monitor screen, and, raising the boom slightly, Clem Jones was able to use them, together with the two rows of strip lights, as aiming marks in Wheelbarrow's move towards the car.

Judging that Wheelbarrow was nearing the car, he was

able, by careful manipulation of the controls, to bring it into position across the centre of the road with the boom now pointing at the car's rear door. Its journey had not been smoothly mechanical—unevenness in the road surface was transmitted to the top hamper of the vehicle, causing the monitor picture to swing away from the target, sometimes wildly, and frozen patches on the road were making the tracks slip.

Andrew Johnston now took over the controls and, slowly and deliberately, advanced Wheelbarrow until he judged that only twelve inches separated the shotgun muzzle from the side of the car. The influence of the camber had now effectively lowered the boom until it was pointed just below the door glass so, operating the boom controls until the shotgun was pointing directly at the centre of the window, he selected the appropriate firing channel and raised the safety guard. With a warning shout, he pressed the firing switch.

The flat sound of the exploding cartridge echoed along the tunnel, followed instantly by the sound of two car door windows shattering—the shot had passed across the car and out through the other window. The picture disappeared off the monitor screen; then, with a flash of light, re-established itself, showing a roughly circular hole the size of his fist in the centre of the crazed, granular window glass. Manipulating the boom, Andrew quickly pushed out the rest of the broken glass.

Further adjustment brought into view a hardboard and wood box, sitting amidst the glass granules scattered over the seat. The box, about the size of a one-pound chocolate box, had two wires, one darker than the other, emerging from its rear to disappear down the crack between the seat cushion and back. Two holes could be seen in the box, one in its side and one in the top, through which he could see the glint of a torch bulb. He was unable to establish, however, whether the wires led to the underside of the seat or into the boot.

Dismounting from the Transit, he saw Bert Smith walking into the station hall. He followed quickly and said, 'Bert, it's a confirmed bomb, but I don't want anybody to move until I give the OK. I need to fire one more shot and everybody must be under cover in case the whole bloody issue goes up. You remember that the threat said that the bomb would explode if the car was moved. I'm worried that there might be a mercury switch in the box, and I don't feel like taking a chance on moving it, not even with Wheelbarrow. We've got to assume something between one hundred and fifty and two hundred pounds of explosive—that would make quite a clatter! It would certainly get rid of the wax in your ears.'

Bert Smith nodded to the inspector who passed the confirmation over the air to MP Mobile, together with a firm warning that anybody coming into the scene, Bomb Squad included, must approach from Lambeth Bridge and remain at Pendennis House. Time: 11.25.

Eight

The detective-constable looked up from answering one of the telephones in Bomb Squad Reserve and remarked to the room in general, 'The car at Vauxhall is confirmed positive!'

Rising from his chair, the duty officer marked up the board and timed the entry, then contacted the action squad so that a team would be sent to the scene. With Greenwich, Holborn, the letter bombs, and now Vauxhall, it was beginning to look as if more people would have to be called in. And, since the correct name for the unit was not 'Bomb Squad' but 'Anti-Terrorist Branch', they were now involved with the Islington hostage situation.

The Chief Superintendent poked his head round the door of the Reserve room, and was brought up to date and asked to authorise reinforcements.

The telephone rang again, to be answered by the constable who, after listening a moment, interrupted the duty officer, saying to the Chief Superintendent, 'Excuse me, guv, Mr Warlock would like to see you in the DAC's office as soon as poss. He sounded in a bit of a hurry.'

Commander Warlock was normally head of the Anti-Terrorist Branch but was acting in place of the Deputy Assistant Commissioner, who was on leave, and, true to form, was working from the more prestigious office.

More than six feet tall, with greying wavy hair, his film-star good looks were marred by cold, hooded eyes. A self-seeking, ambitious slave-driver, he was an ex-paratrooper subaltern, and was unique in being the first Bomb Squad

Commander translated direct from the uniform branch, an interesting experiment in an appointment where detective ability, shrewdness and leadership had, hitherto, been regarded as essential.

Seated behind the DAC's desk, he looked up as the Chief Superintendent knocked on the office door and entered. He did not offer him a seat but brusquely demanded to be given an up-date on Vauxhall and Islington.

'Well, sir, the car at Vauxhall is now confirmed and the Explosives Officer is dealing with it. It will take some time, I'm afraid, and the area is completely closed as well as Waterloo Station.'

'Which one is dealing?'

'Andrew Johnston. He started off at Greenwich, then cleared Liverpool Street before he was called to Vauxhall. The press are starting to gather down there but Press Bureau are covering it.'

'Why is Johnston doing so much?'

'Apart from one being off sick and the one in hospital, the current shift system does not allow much scope for emergencies but, of course, Commander Tech. Support would be better able to explain all that.'

'Well, I'll be going down there shortly myself so I can see what's happening. Now—what's the situation at Islington? Tell me from the start. I shall have to put the ACC in the picture and I want all the angles covered. I don't want him telling me something that I should know already.'

The Chief Superintendent told him the facts, adding that the terrorist's description appeared to be close to the one they had for the man who shot the bank messenger in Warren Street earlier that morning.

'What are we doing there? If it's IRA then it's our scene and I don't want it ruined by the locals.'

'The nearby flats have been evacuated—all of them—the area cordoned off, we've got men and equipment into the next-door flat and the ones above and below. One of our superintendents—a qualified negotiator—is down there with the local commander. It's being played low-key at the moment. We're sitting it out but the marksmen are in position. The media are there.'

No thanks, just a grunt, so the Chief Superintendent left and returned to his own office. Warlock was going to have a job making up his mind with the media at both places at once. It would be interesting to see where he decided to go—always assuming that the ACC gave him the choice.

Andrew Johnston turned to Bert Smith and asked if representatives from British Rail, the buses, the Underground, Police E & M engineering could be got together—here, in the station hall, would be the best place. When this had been set in motion he remarked to the Chief Superintendent, 'You haven't seen our little marvel in action, have you? I've got to do a bit more with it while we're waiting, so, if you want to, you can come and watch on the monitor. I'm thinking of 11.40 for the next stage but we may have to put that back a bit.'

Together, they walked to the Transit and climbed in, Clem Jones moving out of the way. Explaining what he had done up to then, Johnston switched on the monitor and Bert Smith was able to see the inside of the car with the box on the seat in the centre of the picture. Andrew pointed out the test bulb, the arming hole and, particularly, the pair of lead wires, then explained that his main concern was that a mercury switch might be in the box and that he therefore proposed to cut the wires. In response to Bert Smith's look of enquiry, he described the method that he proposed to use.

Then, picking up the control unit, he retracted the boom, then reversed Wheelbarrow to the centre of the road, before taking a new line into the car so that he could shoot out the lead wires and isolate the box. Keeping his eye on the monitor screen he was surprised to detect a movement at its edge, and adjusting the controls, he pointed the camera past the car. To his utter dismay he saw a human figure lurch into view from the direction of an opening in the wall and then, apparently attracted by the bright light, stagger towards Wheelbarrow, holding a quart cider bottle in his right hand.

'Bleeding hell!' said the Chief Superintendent. 'A bloody wino! He must have come out of the milk depot. We're supposed to have cleared everybody out of there!'

Andrew Johnston grabbed his helmet, pulled it on to his head and shot out of the van, along the pavement and around the corner into the tunnel, in a desperate dash towards the car. As he turned the corner he heard a chorus of shouts coming from the direction of The Elephant and Castle, where he saw two policemen waving violently at the man and calling out in alarm.

Reaching him, Andrew was conscious that the unwelcome visitor was standing, swaying as if mesmerised by the boom light, about ten feet away from it. Unkempt, bleary-eyed, unshaven, he wore an indescribably filthy raincoat secured with a length of sash-cord, and the legs of a pair of discoloured blue serge trousers, badly frayed at the rear, flopped over his shabby tennis shoes.

Catching a glimpse of Andrew Johnston dashing towards him through the alcoholic haze, he drunkenly waved the bottle towards Wheelbarrow, swaying and mouthing an incomprehensible, slack-mouthed greeting. Intent on preventing the drunkard from touching the car, Andrew seized him by the arm, becoming aware of an overpowering stench, and feeling thankful that he had slipped on his gloves as he ran forward.

He thrust the man, staggering and sliding, fighting against his grip, mouthing drunken obscenities and trying to use the bottle as a weapon, firmly towards the pub. At the edge of the pavement, the man's left foot, hitting an icy patch, shot forward into the air and he sprawled on the ground, dragging Andrew down across his reeking body. The cider bottle flew through the air in a graceful arc to smash explosively against the slimy wall. Recovering his senses, Andrew struggled to his feet and then, with considerable difficulty, managed to cajole and lift the drunkard from the ground. Getting a good grip on him once again, he propelled him towards the corner and the two advancing policemen.

He followed them to the front of Barclays Bank, where he leaned against its door, gasping for breath, a tremor running up his legs. Taking off his helmet, he realised that his hair was wet through with sweat while his spectacles were sliding down his nose, the lenses obscured by the moisture running down off his forehead. The raw cold of the morning was once more eating its way through his clothing and he shivered. He went down the nearby steps to the Underground station and then, using another tunnel, found himself on the pavement in front of Vauxhall Station booking hall. As he walked through the station hall, Bert Smith and Peter Barwell came to meet him, both smiling. The Chief Superintendent shook him vigorously by the hand and congratulated him on dealing with the drunk so efficiently.

A quick briefing revealed that the various representatives would soon be present, that Bomb Squad were now at Pendennis, together with the Press Bureau and that the system was now fully organised to put everybody under cover when he required it. Andrew Johnston decided that the time had come to cut the leads.

'I'm going to position the Wheelbarrow ready to shoot but I'll wait until you let me know that everybody's secure. I'll get you to broadcast a warning, then give a short countdown, blow my whistle and fire. Nobody is to move before I give the OK. I would like Peter to come with me, if that's all right with you, as I haven't got a radio link and I feel that there should be one.'

Reaching the Transit, he found that Wheelbarrow was still in the middle of the road where he had left it, although Clem Jones had switched everything off to conserve power—the batteries only had limited life and it took a little time to change them. Switching on, Andrew turned to the inspector and said, 'Your cardboard box actually turned out to be made of hardboard and wood, Peter. You'll be able to see it in a minute when we get the boom lined up. There can't have been too much light when you saw it before.'

Just as he was about to move Wheelbarrow a dark shadow appeared at the right of the monitor picture and, gently panning the camera, he saw a black dog which had materialised near the back of the car. The mythical black dog was something of a tradition in the Met, being reported as a significant factor in many otherwise inexplicable traffic accidents involving police vehicles. It was just as well that there were witnesses.

Obviously hearing the noise of the panning motor, the dog, a near-Labrador, lean and unkempt, half-crouched, its nose questing in Wheelbarrow's direction, the whites of its eyes showing in the light. The noise having ceased when the camera came to rest, the dog resumed its search of the area, poking its nose into pieces of paper, sniffing along the wall and pavement, getting even nearer to the car, marking at intervals.

'Don't touch the car, you stupid bloody animal,' breathed Andrew. 'Don't touch the car! It could be the last thing you'll ever bloody do!'

While Andrew considered the advisability of using the shotgun on the dog, it made its inquisitive way around and then, moving towards the rear wheel arch, with a supremely unconscious sense of occasion, set itself firmly, raised its hind leg and, with evident relish, even bliss, marked the rear wheel thoroughly. Satisfied, it trotted away from the car towards Vauxhall Bridge, checking the buses on the way, its step jaunty and its breath misting in the cold air. If dogs could be said to grin this one was doing it.

'Everywhere there's critics,' Andrew remarked, 'but here we don't need them. I'm bloody glad he's gone. He might have done a lot of damage.'

Turning back to the control unit, he took Wheelbarrow slowly forward until, once more, it reached the car door and the view of the inside of the car reappeared on the monitor screen. 'This is the tricky bit,' he explained, 'I've got to get the boom in, then point the shotgun at a pair of wires coming out of the rear of the box. It's got to be done without touching any part of the car—otherwise, if there is a mercury switch, it might be jogged into action. The real trouble is that the camera is stuck up on the top of the boom and you can't watch the back. So you have to try to remember the layout, in three dimensions that is, and then estimate the boom's movement.'

Pressing the various controls in turn, he eased the boom gingerly forward until the box came into view on the monitor. Then, barely touching the buttons and switches, he lined up the shotgun on the wires.

'I want to get the muzzle as close to the wires as I can, Peter. I've got to be certain of hitting them but I want to cut down any danger of the muzzle blast hitting the box before the wires are cut.'

Andrew Johnston inched the boom forward, trying, with all the finesse that he could muster, to get as close as possible. On the screen, he saw the car give the slightest of twitches so he retraced the boom very delicately. Letting out a slow breath, he asked, 'Can you find out how much longer before I can fire? The sooner that we get this next move over, the better—this job's begining to drag on a bit! And when that happens it gets more dangerous.'

Getting out of the van, the inspector went off to find Bert Smith while Andrew, relaxing, chatted with Clem Jones and Len Pound. Stretching himself energetically, he thought, God! It's been a long day, and it's not finished yet! He was beginning to feel chilled and was looking forward to something to drink.

Out of a reflective silence, Clem asked, 'That bomb at Liverpool Street, Andy. Say it had been a real one and not a hoax. How much damage would it have done?'

'Well, for a start we don't know how much explosive there would have been in it or what sort. But the normal size for one of those is about ten pounds and on that assumption, one thing's certain—the Polyfoto box would have gone for a shit.

That's for starters. Then all the stuff in the area—the ticket offices, collectors' boxes, the telephone boxes, the other stuff standing in the hall—all would have been badly mashed up and at least two of the escalators would have been put out of action. I reckon also that there would have been a hole in the floor where it was standing, and I'm pretty certain that the roof above the bomb would have been brought down—and that means there would have been a hole in the ground of the station near the top of the stairs. It could have been quite a big hole. There's no doubt that the station would have had to close for some time.'

Peter Barwell reappeared in the doorway and told him that everybody was under cover and the final warning given.

Andrew shouted the short countdown, blew his whistle, then, lifting the safety guard, pressed the firing switch.

The sound of the cartridge exploding echoed through the tunnel again, to be followed, thankfully, by silence spreading over the whole area, even the background noises seeming to hold their breath. Looking at the monitor he saw that the box had disappeared and, where the wires had been, there was a new jagged hole through the seat, exposing its filling. Time: 11.48.

Setting off on the next mile and three quarters to Putney Bridge, the freezing cold was eating into the Georgious, starting the misery-making process of chilling them to the marrow. Harrods' massive furniture depository with its beflagged twin towers, loomed out of the fog on their right to vanish slowly as they motored on down-river. The river bend was taking them over to the right, away from a stretch of parkland, when Nicos saw, ahead of them, a succession of pleasure boats, mostly cabin cruisers, moored in a line well out from the bank. A feeling of lethargy, induced by the cold, was creeping over him, so that, seeing them late, he had to swing the tiller violently to avoid running into one of the boats. This caused the craft to swing towards the centre of the river and, losing his grip on the throttle, he was forced to make a frantic grab at the softly rounded side of the inflatable to retain his balance. With its engine dead, the craft floated, out of control, spinning slowly along the line of moored cruisers, John and Carlo now crying out in fear. The treat had lost its savour, and danger now occupied every thought, danger and its avoidance.

Scrabbling in the bottom of the craft, Nicos felt the toggle rope under his trembling, icy fingers. The combined effects of intense cold and shock had frozen his powers of thought but, shivering violently, he managed to wind the rope around the starting pulley in the first action of the firing sequence. John and Carlo, reduced to silence in a cub-like appreciation of the futility of further noise, huddled, motionless, staring up at their father as he pulled the toggle sharply towards himself. The depressing result was an apologetic cough followed by a couple of chuffs, then silence—a silence broken by the intruding sound of escaping air. Looking towards the source of this new noise, Nicos saw the rolled-up corner of an old square adhesive patch sticking up in the air from its position on the side of the craft.

Three attempts later, Nicos was delighted to hear the engine splutter into life, and with a shout of encouragement verging on hysteria, he sat down again and, resuming his grip on the throttle, brought the craft once more under control. Turning his attention to the failing patch he told John to roll it out flat and then press his hand on it in an attempt to limit the loss of air.

The period without power had seen them pass under both Putney Bridge and Putney Railway Bridge and, as far as he could judge, the tide was starting to ebb, its pull slowly aiding their speed. His spirits began to rise slightly as he took them under the high centre-span of Wandsworth Bridge.

Commander Macleod was under pressure but he showed not the slightest sign—that wasn't his style. A determined Calvinist, his belief in the message of Hymn 91, A. & M., *Christian, dost thou see them*, was absolute.

The combined weight of the media circus was gathering—the troops of Midian—on the holy ground of Pendennis House, that off-shoot of Scotland Yard. Both denominations of UK television news were there in full force, audio, video, cable humpers, charwallahs, and the papers, local, national, quality, gutter, evening. *Striving, tempting, luring, goading into sin.* The London *Evening Globe* was trying anxiously to get something for the late editions, while the rest of the press was more relaxed because of later deadlines. *How they speak thee fair*. Crowded into a conference room, set aside as a temporary information room, they lacked two essentials—hard information and telephones. Those, and the freedom to go anywhere they pleased, a facility which was second nature to them. A caged media man, unless sleeping or pursuing the active detailed analysis of alcohol tolerance, is likely to develop pressures akin to those in a runaway pressure boiler. *Always watch and prayer*.

One voice broke free of the general level of noise. 'Commander, can you tell us what's going on? One bomb went off at Greenwich early this morning, then there was a hoax at Liverpool Street and the shooting at Praed Street and now there's this lot here!'

'I'm afraid that I have no information on incidents that occur outside my district and I'm sure that you are all aware of that. I am not in a position to make any statement on the situation here yet.'

'Oh! For Christ's sake, Commander! We've got to have news—it's our right. It's our job. When can we get nearer to this car—it is a car, isn't it?' The pressure was rising under the influence of this Judas Goat—the omnipresent, self-appointed big mouth, pursuing the unilaterally assumed credo of the fourth estate.

The conference room door opened to admit a small group of men—an obvious PR-oriented policeman with an indefinable pair of companions. They moved up to the head of the room amid a sudden silence—irritation, curiosity, recognition, anticipation were all components. Setting himself in the approved posture, the policeman spoke, 'Good morning, ladies and gentlemen. Some of you know me but, for the benefit of those who do not, I am Commander Pat Warlock, head of the Bomb Squad. Today I'm acting DAC Ops.'

Pat Warlock spoke in the practised manner of a natural declaimer. After accepting for years the previous official policy of a Trappist approach to the press, he was now revelling in the opportunity to cultivate a TV image. The road to the stars, or at least a plum job on retirement, was now beckoning. Speaking directly to the staring eyes of the whirring cameras, the focus of caged Zeppelin-like microphones, he continued, 'The car has been confirmed as a bomb and the threat substantiated, so I'm going forward to check on the current position. When I have done that I shall let you know what is happening—I shall speak to you again, here, at, hopefully, 12.30. Now, while I am gone, these two gentlemen, whom I am sure you all recognise come from the Press Department, will answer your questions and do their best to help you.'

With the air of purpose that he had cultivated as part of his outward personality, he swept out of the room.

Commander Macleod also left, determined to preserve the air of reason in the proceedings at the scene—it was, after all, his patch. As he passed the door of MP Mobile, the Inspector stuck his head out and called, 'Commander Macleod, sir, there's a message that you ought to know about. The Deputy Commissioner has said that the Home Secretary or his Minister of State may visit the scene after lunch. It is possible that the matter may be raised in the House this afternoon.'

'Thank you very much, Inspector. I'd be obliged if you did not pass that information on inside. If any more on that comes in, let me know, but only me. I'm going down to see Mr Smith now and should be there for some time.'

Walking away, Macleod mused, 'We can do without that. It's probably only a fence-mending operation to gather ammunition to be used in the eternal talking battle over the river. Something difficult must be in the offing—there must be need for a diversion. Let's hope that Andrew Johnston really knows what he is doing! A lot can depend on his clearing this properly. The real problem will arise with Warlock and the media. Once they get a whiff of any visit it will be worse here than the scramble to get tickets for the Calcutta Cup at Murrayfield! I'm pretty certain that I saw some Americans among the press, too. I ought to have a quiet word with those two from Press Bureau.'

The cold was still intense but the whisper of a breeze seemed to be causing the fog to lighten. Certainly the vision distance seemed to have become greater but maybe it was because he had been inside the building for a long while; it could be an illusion.

The buzz of the switchboard alarm attracted Detective-Sergeant Brockway's attention away from his cup of tea and he picked up the operator's handset.

'This is Commander Butler. What's the latest at Vauxhall?'

'Good morning, sir.' Conrad Butler was Commander, Tech. Support at the Yard. 'We've just had confirmation that it's a car bomb. Bomb Squad have been informed and the media are at Pendennis. Andrew Johnston is reviewing the situation with the local commander before trying to neutralise.'

'Chief Superintendent Gregory is on his way to you—ask him to ring me at my office when he arrives, please. What are the others up to?'

'Frank Norrie's just cleared at Oxford Street—it was a good hoax. He's going on to a couple of suspect letters at Kilburn Sorting Office, and Don Reynolds is still out at Theobalds Road.'

'What's there?'

'A carrier bag in the yard at Lacon House, an MOD building. There was a threat on that one as well. It was coded.'

'Thank you very much, Sergeant. I'll be here if anybody wants me. I'm having lunch in the building, but the phone will be manned.'

Replacing his handset, Nigel Brockway leaned back in his

chair and turned up the volume on the Force radio set, listening to the traffic. With the major incident at Vauxhall and the other calls outstanding, the message channel had now been allocated solely for bomb reports. If it kept up like this he was going to need some help, with the telephones to man as well as the radio.

He reached for the telephone as the buzzer sounded again.

'Hello, Nigel, this is Hilary Grey. Can you tell me anything about the accident this morning? I've just heard about it on the radio. Which one was involved? How bad is it?'

'Hallo, Hilary. Nice to hear from you. This morning's incident involved Joe Hawke, I'm afraid. He's in hospital at Woolwich—pretty bad I'm sorry to say. Fiona has been to see him and should be at home by now. How are the children?'

'Oh, they're fine. What happened to Joe?'

Nigel Brockway gave her a brief résumé of the facts as he knew them. Hilary was in a specially privileged position and was genuinely concerned with the continuing welfare of the Explosives Officers. She was the widow of the only Explosives Officer to have been killed on operations—murdered by a terrorist bomb—leaving her with two children, a boy and a girl, to educate and raise. A small, slim woman of considerable attraction she was engaged in charity work as a personal reparation to the public who, through the medium of the police service and a public subscription, were caring so generously for her and her family.

'Thank you, Nigel. I'll telephone Fiona later. She will probably need some help, particularly from an old friend.'

The buzzer on the front door lock sounded loudly in the silence and, having checked through the window, Zoe Black, the female clerk, pressed the release button. Bernard Gregory walked along the corridor and, entering the communications room, greeted Nigel, who told him about the Commander's message.

'Give me one of the office lines, Sergeant. I'll call him now.' He dialled. 'Hullo, sir, Bernard Gregory here. I've just come over from my office. I was at the hospital earlier. Joe Hawke has rather less than an even chance, but they're doing everything humanly possible and a bit more. His wife has been taken home—she's pretty calm, rather too calm. There's a WPC with her in case she needs help. I've sent his driver off—he was on night duty and should have been home anyway.'

'That's a point! Who's taking over nights?'

'Well, Johnston, Norrie, Reynolds and Parry-Evans are on now, and Maby is sick—it looks like Blair.'

'OK. You tell him. He'll have to take over for the rest of the week. Now, about Vauxhall—have you been down there yet? It's been confirmed.'

'No, sir. I haven't. I didn't know about the confirmation. I'll go and see what's happening.'

'Keep me in the picture, Bernard. I've got to keep the fifth floor happy and this job looks like it might cause some outside interest. Pretty high level interest, I'll bet.'

Signing off, Gregory thought that instead of keeping them happy it would be better if the Commander could keep most of them away from the scene. Tourists were always a pain in the backside at these affairs—always trying to give the impression that their presence was the only thing ensuring success. With Johnston on the scene there could be some bizarre comments—he had a name for plain speaking.

He picked up the coffee which Zoe had made and sipped it slowly, and then, carrying it into the communications room, looked through the messages. Nothing wildly exciting—five outstanding, all postal items, which could wait. He asked, 'Is the second Wheelbarrow operational?'

'No, sir. It's in workshops for modification. It'll be in for several days, so the one at Vauxhall is all we've got available.'

'Right. I'm going there shortly. Meanwhile get in touch with Hamish Blair and tell him he's on tonight, and the rest of the week.'

'That's a pity, guv. He's the one most likely to make a fuss.'

'He can object all he likes! The job comes first. In any case, it's the Commander's orders.'

Brockway picked up the phone. Bernard Gregory sat down and finished his coffee then telephoned his own office—no new problems—and told them where he could be found.

'Hamish Blair would like a word with you, guv,' Brockway said.

'Chief Superintendent Gregory here.'

'Bernard, I'm afraid that I can't swap duties. I've got a previous engagement that I don't want to break.'

'Look—you are aware what's happened, aren't you? About Joe Hawke? You're due for night duty next week anyway and it is an emergency.'

'I know that, but I'm afraid it's impossible. My arrangements are firm and they've been made for a long while. Everybody in the office knew about them.'

'Well, Hamish, I'm afraid that the incident at Greenwich was not foreseen and this is an emergency. Joe didn't do it just to spite you or muck up your arrangements. The Commander has approved the change. Shall I show you as refusing duty?'

There was a long silence, which Bernard Gregory allowed to run on, before Blair, obviously unhappy, grudgingly agreed to the change.

To Brockway, Bernard Gregory uttered the classic phrase, 'He's having it!'

Nine

Drained temporarily of all tension, Andrew Johnston leaned back on the temporary seat, eased his cramped muscles and smiled happily at Peter Barwell, sitting beside him.

'How about that then? It's nice to see something going according to plan! Mind you, Peter, we've still got the rest to deal with, but if there was any trembler in that car it's gone now. Will you give your guv'nor the OK, and I'll be around in a couple of minutes.'

As the duty officer climbed out of the Transit, Andrew turned to Clem Jones. 'Well? They don't teach you that at Hendon, you bloody turkey. You've got to agree—that was sheer poetry—magic!'

'So? It bloody well ought to be—after all I've taught you. But, seriously, Andy, it was a damned fine job. Now you've got the rest to do. Do you want Wheelbarrow moved back?'

'No, Clem, leave it there for now. You know, when the cartridge goes off and nothing else happens it's a bit of an anti-climax. Although you feel confident that you've got it all wrapped up and the only sound will be that of the shot, you're always tensed up ready for the whole lot to go up with a bloody great bang.'

The banter between them was part of a well-rehearsed wind-down procedure. Leaving the van, Andrew set off for the station hall, reflecting and analysing as he went . . . *No mercury switch—if there was a time switch in the box, it's finished now . . . what possibilities are left? Concealed time mechanism? . . . Anti-removal mechanisms in the explosive charge? . . . Something connected to the doors? . . . Anti-opening mechanism in the boot lid? The bonnet? . . . There's still a lot to do . . . could take some time . . .*

The group in the station entrance was in earnest discussion, with Andrew taking the leading part. Apart from Bert Smith and Peter Barwell there were representatives from British Rail, London Tranport, the Underground, Thames Water Authority, SEGAS, SEEBOARD, the Post Office and a senior member of the local Chief Engineer's Department—everybody with an interest in the situation. On a newly swept area of the floor Andrew Johnston had chalked out a rough plan of the area and was going over the actions that he had taken and the choices which he saw for the future.

'As you all know, early this morning the Consort under the railway was the subject of a threat. It was claimed to be a car bomb which would explode if any attempt was made to move it. Since then we've got into the car with Wheelbarrow and killed the control box, which I estimate may have contained a timer and a mercury switch. We're all uncomfortably aware that nearly three hours have elapsed since the threat, but you can't hurry these things.'

'I appreciate that you have problems, Major, but, as far as the railway is concerned, we've got nothing moving in or out of Waterloo main-line. Trains from this station serve Berkshire, Hampshire and the West Country as well as commuters from South-West London, Middlesex and Surrey. That's an awful lot of passengers! The Underground is running through without stopping, as you know, and the buses have been rerouted, but we are getting on towards the afternoon rush and the fog isn't helping. It won't simply be a matter of changing a few signals and away—there's got to be a lot of re-planning before the first train can run on this line. The railway is a very complicated interlocking system timed to the minute.' This was the Vauxhall Station Manager, an intense, experienced man who, nevertheless, carried the responsibility of his job easily.

'Well, I think it's my duty to say that, whatever method is adopted, the scene cannot be released for at least an hour. It is possible, of course, that it could be longer but that depends on a number of things. But, to continue, the fact that I have managed to deal with the control box doesn't mean that all the problems have disappeared. It is still not certain that we can move the car safely or that there's not another timer. Assuming that I find that I can move the car, it might be the best idea to drag it away from where it is, in the hope that the railway can start up again.'

The sound of footsteps from the Lambeth Road end announced the arrival of the Deputy Borough Engineer and, after he had introduced himself, Andrew quickly brought him up to date. The newcomer lost no time in entering the discussion. 'Where were you thinking of moving the car, Major?' he asked. 'How much explosive are we talking about?'

'To answer the second question first, up to two hundred pounds.'

'What will it do if it goes off? What will be the effect on the bridge—the railway bridge, that is?'

'There would be serious damage to it. In my opinion the steelwork will be lifted at least, and the brickwork will suffer badly. For the rest, the buses will be destroyed, the pub and the bank will be badly knocked about, and there will be a crater in the pavement, and God knows what's under there. The Langley Lane area is in the blast and missile zone and right up to Bridgefoot will be covered with debris. It won't be a pretty sight and will take a long time to clear up. Now, to deal with the other question, the problem of where to move the car. Let me say first that it won't be on to Vauxhall Bridge, but it's got to be somewhere pretty near, somewhere that doesn't mean moving too far. Under these conditions, the places which might be possible are Wandsworth Road, the Albert Embankment, Lambeth Road or Nine Elms Lane, but, obviously, there are going to be factors that I don't know about, and that's what we're here for—to find out the difficulties and to help me decide on the best course. The one thing that I must point out is that if the car is dragged to any road running alongside the railway, it doesn't mean that the trains can start again. If the car detonated while a train was passing there would be an absolute disaster. Two hundred pounds means a lot of blast and there's a great deal of metal in a car.'

The London Transport representative spoke up. 'To deal specifically with Wandsworth Road—we have the station booking hall under the lorry park and Bridgefoot, with passenger-access tunnels from a number of directions, some on this side of the road. In addition, the Victoria Line runs underneath and is still operating.'

While he had been talking, a police sergeant had come in from Lambeth Road to speak quietly to Peter Barwell who immediately passed on some information to the Chief Superintendent. Seizing his opportunity when the Underground man had made his point, Bert Smith broke in: 'We seem to have another pretty urgent problem, Major! One of my men has found what looks like a second bomb on the bridge, and we want you to look at it.'

They moved away from the group before he continued, 'Chained to the railings on the left-hand side of the bridge, right next to the first pier, there is a vehicle counter box. At least, it looks like one, but there's something unusual about it. My sergeant here has seen it, so it would be better if he tells you himself.'

'Well, sir, it's the normal sort of box, chained up and with the rubber pipe fixed out into the road but there's a wire coming out of the back and going over the side of the bridge and disappearing underneath. One chap said he could hear ticking, but I couldn't myself.'

'So it's the wire that's worrying everybody, is it. Nothing else?'

'Yes, sir, that and the ticking.'

'Right, I'll have a look at the problem. Could I see it from the lorry park, do you think?'

'I think so—providing you select your position and use bins.'

Returning to the now silent group, Andrew Johnston excused himself, promising to be back as soon as possible and asking them to consider the matter further in his absence so that it would be easier to make a later decision. Time: 12.00.

London, today, has been the scene of a number of violent incidents with apparent Irish links. Very early this morning an explosion at the Royal Naval College in Greenwich resulted in a police explosives officer being seriously injured. A telephone call, reputed to be from the Irish National Liberation Army, claimed responsibility for placing a bomb there. Later, the Underground train service at Liverpool Street station was disrupted for nearly two hours by a hoax device believed to have been placed by the same organisation . . . In mid-morning, a man was shot and killed in Warren Street, but the gunman escaped before he could be apprehended . . . At Islington, a gunman, claiming to be a member of the Provisional IRA, has taken a woman and her two children hostage and it is thought that these two incidents may be connected . . . The area of Vauxhall Cross is at a standstill and no trains are moving in or out of Waterloo Station because of a large car bomb which has been found in the area after a call received from the Provisional IRA. Explosives experts are now engaged in trying to defuse this bomb but Scotland Yard state that they are unable to tell how long this will take . . . Meanwhile, in Northern Ireland, seven large bombs have exploded during the morning in Belfast, Omagh, Newry . . . Today is the first anniversary of the death of Bobby Monaghan, the hunger striker . . . Today also sees the publication of the Northern Ireland Assembly Bill which has given rise to so much controversy and is due to be debated in Parliament within . . .

* * *

The rum was finished—long ago—but McAllister's craving was not. To an alcoholic like him the limited supplies of hard booze in the flat only emphasised his deprivation.

The children weren't helping either, terror, hunger and their total inability to understand what was going on combining to produce a chorus of whimpering and sobbing punctuated only by shuddering exhaustion. Their mother's despairing fear, twisting up her insides and gnawing away at her composure was manifesting itself in a constant restlessness. Increasing her terror further was his insistence that one child remain with him at all times.

The flat was now very cold, for he refused to allow her to make up the fire—he was sweating as it was and could see no reason to worry about anybody else's comfort. Sitting in an upright chair, sunk in melancholy, his fingers drumming on the table, he started up as the raucous, metallic sound of a loud-hailer penetrated the window from the street.

Snatching up his gun from the table, he advanced towards the window, bawling at Janice Leroy to move forward as well. The sudden noise caused both children to scream hysterically, making her turn back instinctively in their direction. McAllister's reaction was instantaneous. Roaring at her to get to the window, his eyes bulging with rage, he thumbed back the hammer and pointed the automatic straight at the three-year-old, the trigger finger knuckle whitening.

The two children now terrified into complete silence, all four figures froze into an obscene tableau, broken, after what seemed a lifetime, by Janice screaming at the top of her voice, 'Don't shoot! Oh, don't shoot! I'll do anything you want. I'm going to the window. Just don't shoot!' Breaking into heart-rending sobs, tears streaming down her face, she rushed to the window where she stood, shaking uncontrollably, facing the Glaswegian.

Like a man coming out of a trance, he slowly released his pressure on the trigger and hissed, 'That's your last chance, you bloody stupid bitch! You better believe it! Any more stupid bloody moves from you or them outside and he gets it! Then it will be the wean and then you! I'm not bloody kidding. Now, open the window, you stupid woman.'

The policemen in the flat upstairs and the one next door relaxed and resumed their seats, replacing their weapons on the floor. After the occupants of these flats had been evacuated, men and equipment had been moved in to set up surveillance. Sensitive listening devices had been successfully and quickly installed but this success had not yet been achieved with a video system. The ring of police containment was completed by the presence of two armed men on the landing, one on each side of the front door, and another on each of the landings, all with their weapons ready and cocked, alert for instant action. Every man was equipped with personal radio.

When the window's lower half had been fully raised, the loud-hailer's harsh voice trumpeted across the street, 'Mrs Leroy, this is the police speaking. Are you all right? Are your children all right?' Receiving a satisfactory although nearly inaudible reply, the voice continued, 'Is there anything you want?'

Before she could reply, McAllister's brutal tones interrupted, 'Just tell him that unless they do what I want, I'm going to shoot the three of you in turn. Tell him that!'

She relayed the message, her voice gaining in strength. Contact with the police, albeit long-range and purely vocal, was imbuing her with hope, however faint.

'Before we answer that, would the man allow us to supply a telephone so that we can talk to him direct?'

''Ere, sarge, how long's this lot going on, then? I'm due for my refs and there's no sign of a relief!'

'Buggered if I know, son, I only work here!'

Refs, refreshments, the break allowed to street policemen, amounts almost to a religious belief in Trafpol and missing them was a catastrophe of mammoth proportions.

'What's it all about then? Why are we here anyway? All I

know is that Traffic Control diverted me here to report to you and we're still here. God, it's perishing, positively taters!'

'There's a car bomb under the bridge at Vauxhall Cross and no trains or vehicles are being allowed in the area. So there's plenty of stops out diverting the traffic. One of the explosives officers is working on it now but there's no telling how long it will take.'

The two policemen with their riding breeches, long boots and short, belted jackets, were very obviously members of Traffic Department, known to most as 'Trafpol'. Wearing their blue peaked caps meant that the white protective helmets had to be parked somewhere safe, so they were resting on the saddles of the powerful BMWs, their radios giving tongue in the open air, standing across the middle of Wandsworth Road at its junction with Wilcox Street.

With the normal commuter traffic using the main road as a speedway even in the fog it was as well that they were wearing the lime-green fluorescent jackets to make them more conspicuous. There was a limit to the number of times that you could leap for your life successfully, particularly on a frosty road. At least the jackets increased the number.

'We'll give it another twenty minutes, son, and then I'll gee them up. With a day like this there can't be many blokes around spare for reliefs.'

'OK, sarge, but you can bet that all the bloody offices are manned. Those buggers won't be coming out in this, not the nine-to-five brigade. God! I'm getting bloody hungry!'

'There's always somebody worse off, you know. That bloke up there is out in the cold as well as working on the bomb, don't forget.'

'That's true. I wouldn't do their bloody job for all the money! I don't know why they do it. They've got to be bloody crackers!'

Leaving the tunnel, Andrew Johnston asked Len Pound to bring Wheelbarrow back to the Transit, then clambered into the Range Rover and, using the same route as previously,

Clem Jones drove him to the lorry park office, and on to the river's edge, using a roundabout route because of the uneven ground. Having unloaded his helmet, spotter 'scope and personal radio, Andrew settled down behind the remains of a brick wall, previously part of a warehouse, telling Clem to take the Range Rover back to the lorry park office away from the danger area.

Setting up the 'scope on the low wall, he pointed it in the direction of the first pier before devoting himself to a study of the bridge's general structure. Made up of five arches with an approach road at each end, the centre of the bridge was noticeably higher than either river bank. The abutments where each span met its neighbour took the form of a vertical steel box column standing on a stone pier, fronted by a large corroded bronze figure of an allegorical nature. Fixed to the top of the pier was a metal bracket bearing navigation lights, while a large, horizontal, painted metal grille made a platform big enough to stand on.

The roadway was supported on these spans, each a shallow orange-painted metal arch with a coupling to the abutments at the ends. Rising up from the pavement was a line of metal railings above a deep tube which bulged out over the river, and between the tube and the top of the arch were vertical white girders which became progressively shorter as they neared the crown of each arch, disappearing entirely over the centre third.

Focusing on the junction of the first and second arches, Johnston could make out the top of the counter box where it just showed above the base of the railings. Dropping down from this he could see an orange coloured cable disappearing into the space between two of the vertical girders, and there, dimly through the fog, he could just glimpse a dark bundle. Whatever the menace, it could not be examined from the shore, or from a boat, and Wheelbarrow would be of no use—the only way would have to be over the railings.

He called Clem to come forward, and then reflected on the significance of what he had seen and heard about the situation . . . *A bundle . . . could mean a hundred pounds or more . . . Orange cable—cable or detonating cord? . . . The ticking could mean delayed arming or a time bomb . . . A hundred-pound bomb could be more than enough to put the bridge completely out of action . . .*

The Range Rover's return interrupted this train of thought. Gathering his gear together, he moved back to the lorry park office where, before leaving, he advised the Superintendent and his team that, in all probability, they would have to move out. Time: 12.15.

Back at the Transit, he found Wheelbarrow ready to be driven up its ramps, and, asking Len Pound to stand fast, he went into the station entrance where he found two distinct groups. Still standing around the chalk plan, the party of experts was obviously continuing its discussion about the car bomb while, some yards away, the group consisted of the Acting DAC, Commander Macleod, Bert Smith, Peter Barwell and, just arrived, Bernard Gregory. From the frozen attitudes of this latter tableau as they looked towards him, Andrew Johnston divined that Pat Warlock had been in full flood, centre stage.

Without waiting for the Explosives Officer to get near, Warlock called out impatiently, 'What's the answer? Is it another one?'

Deliberately waiting until he joined the group, Andrew replied, 'I've been down to the edge of the river and had a look. There's a large bundle pushed under the bridge which must be a bomb—anyway, that's how I'm classifying it.'

Warlock broke in, evidently trying to rush his fences as usual: 'I want to bring the media down here so that they can see what the situation is. They're beginning to get very jumpy stuck back at Pendennis and Force policy is for us to cooperate.'

'Policy makers rarely come to this type of scene,' commented Andrew rather sourly. 'I'm afraid there's no way that I can allow them here—it's too dangerous. There's up to two hundred pounds of high explosive in one place, and now a possible hundred in the other. In any case, I'm going to have to ask you all to leave here because of the direct line of an explosion from the second device into this tunnel.' What he did not say was that valuable time would be wasted in the exercise, nor did he mention the ever-present suspicion of a man in his position that, with their cameras and prying, some relaxation of security would result in greater danger to himself and others engaged in the same work.

'Where do you suggest that we move to, Major?' Macleod enquired.

Warlock opened his mouth to speak but Andrew beat him to the punch. 'I appreciate that it's not actually under cover but I suggest that you move to the pavement on this side of Lambeth Road—that will give you maximum protection from both directions, from both devices. I've still got to look at the second one from close up. Wheelbarrow can't be used, for a number of perfectly valid reasons, the most important of which is that the cable is not long enough to give operator-safety if the thing went up.'

'What about these chaps?' Macleod nodded his head towards the other group. 'They can't stay here, either, can they?'

'No, the risk is the same for everybody. I'll have a word with them.'

Walking over to the other party, he quickly briefed them on the fresh development and the need for them to move to a place of greater safety. Before the conversation ended, however, they advanced their joint view that to move the car would be likely to create more problems than it would solve. Even after moving it the trains could not be restarted until the railway people were satisfied that it had been fully neutralised, while the Underground facilities would be at greater risk. Gas and water mains, electric cables and telephone systems would all present problems in isolating the risk as well as restoring them if it all went wrong.

Andrew Johnston cut short the discussion. 'Gentlemen, we've got to push ahead with the one under the bridge—

Vauxhall Bridge, that is—so I must ask you all to leave now. Your advice and comments have both been extremely helpful — I needed them and certainly couldn't have done without them. I would like to talk to you again, later. Many thanks for coming.'

He turned to Bert Smith and his inspector. 'My safest and best route on to the bridge will be through the pedestrian tunnels across to Bridgefoot and then along the pavement so that I can get a good look at the box. Can you keep all your people under cover and pass the word to the other side of the river? The chaps over there would be at risk as well. Why is it that on jobs like this there's always a boundary running through the scene? We can do without that form of embuggeration! Peter, could you keep your eye on me until I reach the box? When I start operations there I'll give you a wave so that you can get your head down. Then, if anything happens on my way forward, somebody will be able to get going without delay.' Time: 12.35.

Leaving Wandsworth Bridge on the northward curve of the river, Nicos could discern the massive bulk of Fulham Power Station, its stark outlines softened by the fog. The sweep of the current took the inflatable and its crew, their enthusiasm visibly ebbing away, towards Westland Heliport on the Battersea side, where, standing on its pad on the pier, he could just distinguish a helicopter. Ahead, its dirty grey bulk almost hidden in the grey fog, he could pick out the outline of Battersea Railway Bridge, carrying its trains across the river on five spans.

Gingerly edging the craft back into the centre of the river, he was able to steer it between the massive granite piers under the centre span and then, with Charrington's fuel oil point on the one hand and London Underground's Lots Road Power Station on the other, they travelled towards the humped centre of Battersea Bridge with its Indian style fretted panels.

Some minutes later, swinging wide to the left, the inflatable became entangled in the paired circular piers of the ageing

Albert Bridge. Extricating it from this near calamity, Nicos tiptoed slowly past another line of moored vessels off the Chelsea Embankment, aware all the time of the losing battle that John was fighting against the leak. The inflatable was very steadily settling further in the water.

Carlo had been silent for some time now and, looking at him, Nicos could see that he was shivering violently, his hands locked on to the handles of the grip, staring fixedly past John at his father's face. John, occupied with his fight against the leak, was hunched down with his back towards Nicos, giving the impression of total absorption in the task. Battersea Festival Gardens passed foggily on the right, dimly visible, with the Festival Pier, locked and unused, its floating pontoon, bailey bridge roadway and twin square wooden towers poking out from the river bank.

Ten

The Pakington Street tableau had been put together, quietly and professionally, with the skill born of much practice, lengthy debate and experience. Vehicles, four-wheeled as well as two-, had all adopted the silent approach routine, shedding their complements outside the cordon. The build-up had been steady, relentlessly steady, bringing in local uniform and CID, Special Patrol Group, anti-terrorist, Trafpol, marksmen, communications specialists, photographers—cine, video and still—engineers, press liaison and canteen service.

Only functional personnel had been allowed to take up positions inside the taped area of the inner cordon, moving as little as possible, their attention wholly concentrated on the Leroy's flat.

The tension inside the flat was teetering towards complete breakdown. Janice had managed, with some degree of finesse, to prepare enough food and drink for her children to become drowsy, edging towards sleep. Her own terror, however, was undiminished, pervading her body and filling her thoughts as she prayed fervently that neither child would precipitate disaster.

McAllister, for whom inactivity, particularly when it was alcohol-free, was sheer purgatory, interspersed his spells at the table with longer periods spent prowling around the flat like a caged animal. Some instinct of self-preservation kept him away from the windows, however, while he tried desperately to resolve the matter of the telephone. His deep-rooted suspicion of any offer of help from the police was fighting his braggart's desire to transmit a boastful message to his public.

He interrupted his pacing to stand in front of the mother and, towering menacingly over her as she sat at the table, he snarled, 'What did he say about the telephone, woman?'

Starting back in surprise, she quavered, 'He just asked if you wanted a telephone so that you could speak to them direct.'

'Who was he?'

'I couldn't see. It was just a voice.'

'Well, you stupid bitch, get over to that window and tell them I want one. And no tricks mind, I've still got the gun and I'll shoot the boy if you don't behave!'

Trembling with fear, she went across to the window, opened it and stood there in full view, waiting.

Her appearance caused a stir among the watchers, and a lone figure stepped forward holding a loud-hailer. Raising it to his mouth he asked, 'Can I help you, Mrs Leroy? Is there anything that you want?' Her tremulous reply barely carried across the road, 'He wants a telephone.'

'If you watch the window, one will be lowered to you in a bag, already connected. You can take it out of the bag and there will be enough cable for you to take it inside. Are you and the children all right?'

Before she could answer, McAllister's calloused hand stretched out from the shelter of the wall and snatched her away from the window.

Within minutes, a bulky carrier bag appeared from above, to come to rest within reach of the open window, swaying gently on the end of a length of rope. McAllister could see that it contained a bulky, angular object and that a cable also led upwards beside the rope. For fully a minute he stared at it, then he motioned her towards the window again.

Drawing the carrier bag into the room, Janice lifted the telephone clear and placed it on the floor while McAllister covered her with his automatic. Any hopes that he might have entertained of unrestricted access to the nation's telephone system were dashed when he looked at it. Instead of the neat GPO model that he had envisaged he saw an Army field telephone. It was connected directly to the incident control centre.

His eyes fixed on the instrument, as though mesmerised, he gave a violent start when the bell rang sharply once; and then again.

Clad in helmet, bomb jacket and weatherproof, Andrew Johnston left the station tunnel by the booking office and ducked quickly down the steps into the pedestrian tunnel, heading towards the Underground station concourse. The tunnel was as silent as the grave, but much less tidy, the strong odour of urine wafting up at intervals. Emerging into the concourse, he came upon two police officers standing talking quietly to a ticket collector. Telling them as much as he felt necessary, he cautioned them to remain below and keep with them anybody else who appeared. Selecting the appropriate exit by the simple method of reading the directional signs, he found himself moving up the ramp leading to Bridgefoot.

Emerging between two brick walls bounding the ramp, his attention was immediately drawn to the grey-painted metal footbridge leading from the pavement across the width of Bridgefoot towards Camelford House. Had anybody checked that? He supposed somebody had. Although it was intensely cold and crackly underfoot, the fog had lifted reluctantly but perceptibly and he could see that his way ahead was up the pavement climbing steadily in front of him.

Hugging the tall painted plywood fence to his left, Johnston walked purposefully upwards towards the centre of the bridge, quickly reaching the massive granite block, with its VAUXHALL BRIDGE chiselled out and highlighted in gold paint, indicating the start of the bridge proper. From there, a solid stone wall led him to the top of the metal column, some ten feet wide and two feet thick, which rose from the start of the first span.

Running his gaze along the base of the metal railings which had now succeeded the stone wall, he saw the blue-painted counter box chained to them and standing innocently on the paving slabs. With its rubber tube pinned down and stretching across the pavement and out into the road, it would not normally invite a second glance. Merging into the background, part of the scenery, the box would have remained undetected but for a questioning police officer's eyes alighting upon it at a time of abnormal suspicion.

Having no other choice, he advanced on the box. Reaching it, he turned and waved to Peter Barwell, now in the entrance to Kennington Road, before squatting down for a closer examination. The box, eighteen inches high, one foot wide, and nine inches deep, had a stout metal handle on each side through which passed the padlocked steel chain. Threaded on through the railings, the chain anchored the box firmly in position. Up to then everything appeared perfectly normal

With the tide speeding the Georgious under the large centre span of Chelsea Bridge at an ever-increasing rate, a series of dry coughs signalled another engine failure—the fuel tank, very plainly, was empty. Silent once more, the leak gaining ground, the craft was swept farther on under the centre span of Grosvenor Bridge, passing dangerously close to the right-hand boat-shaped stone pier. Moving clear of the bridge, the silence was rent by the rattling, clanking roar of a crowded, away-day train on its way through the fog from the Sussex coast.

Water was seeping in at the bottom of the craft now. It was clear that the leaking patch was not the only failure, for that, after all, was on top of the inflated side, so there must be a weakness in the join between the base and the sides. Carlo, the seat of his jeans icily wet, started to cry, a thin sobbing sound which triggered a violent reaction from John, whose own fear was in serious danger of destroying his older-brother calm.

To Nicos, the silent, spinning craft was now obviously at

the absolute mercy of the ebbing tide, powerless and with no way of steering, destined to follow the centre line of the river until it sank in the freezing water. It had ceased to be a long-awaited treat some time ago, it had ceased to be any sort of pleasure, and had become a dangerous nightmare.

Glen's rear end was in constant motion, his tail semaphoring his delight from side to side under Dave Fox's watchful eye, the dog's weight thrust solidly forward against the lead as he probed into the cardboard box. With a nagging suspicion that there might be another device in the area, Andrew Johnston had requested a dog search outside the inner cordon. Four dogs were now engaged in clearing the area, sniffing at everything and anything.

His handler guided Glen farther along the pavement, the dog snorting and sniffing through rubbish collected in the angle of a wall, sneezing occasionally as disturbed dust got up his nose. A dog with a mind of his own, when his handler tried to dislodge him before he was ready, he just returned and finished the sniffing to his own satisfaction, before continuing, questing and huffing at anything that took his nose, whether at ground level or above his head, occasionally standing tall on his hind legs.

Around the corner they came upon a locked and unattended Morris van standing at the kerbside. The handler unleashed the dog for him to orbit the vehicle, sniffing the edges of all doors and poking his head into the wheel arches. At one particular point at the rear of the van Glen came to a breath-taking halt, sniffing delicately, then moved away, and returned again two or three times, sniffing sensitively, before leaving to pursue his quest elsewhere.

Stepping back into cover after Andrew Johnston's signal, Peter Barwell caught sight of a slight movement on top of Camelford House. Only a flutter seen from the corner of his eye, he was still sure, with a paratrooper's certainty, that somebody was up there. Somebody with no right to be there, trying to stay concealed in a position overlooking Andrew as he worked on the box—a perfect sniper position, with the Explosives Officer at his mercy.

His first impulse was to get a warning to Johnston in some way, but he decided against it in view of the insubstantial nature of the sighting. Not a man to ignore the threat entirely, however, he passed a message to MP Mobile, which resulted in Special Patrol Group despatching four armed men to the roof. While they were making their way to the roof Peter Barwell was walking very smartly around to the Range Rover.

Clem Jones lost no time in calling Andrew on his personal radio and he immediately pivoted round at the crouch to look up at the roof. Even through his helmet visor he at once picked out a man's head, near the river end of the parapet, peering along something too small to make out at that distance. Without waiting to establish further details, Johnston sprinted across the bridge to shelter behind the box column directly opposite.

With drawn revolvers, the four officers stole catlike through one of the doors to the roof of Camelford House to find the kneeling figure, back towards them, completely engrossed in the situation on Vauxhall Bridge. Beside him, on the tarmac, a large Samsonite case, large enough to accommodate a disassembled rifle and sight. As they spread into a tactical, mutually supporting pattern, designed to cover the man whichever way he turned, the sergeant ordered, in a quiet, flat, determined voice, brooking no argument, 'Do not turn round, mister! Don't move. Just stay where you are without moving your hands. We're police officers and we are armed!'

The kneeling man jerked in surprise, a reflex movement quickly stilled by a further sharp command. Advancing cautiously upon the man, two of the officers, their revolvers pointed unwaveringly at him, cocked and ready for instant action, made him stand up, facing out over the parapet. It was immediately obvious that the object he had been aiming was nothing more lethal than a camera fitted with a telephoto lens.

It was a matter of minutes before the Samsonite case was cleared and the man established as a free-lance photographer trying to scoop his fellows. For his pains, his initiative was going to earn him a very uncomfortable half-hour or more, explaining just how he had got there and why he was breaking the agreement not to take pictures of an explosives officer.

With the inflatable now moving inexorably towards Vauxhall, Nicos could see a police boat, hugging the river bank in the distance, just past Battersea Power Station. On the other side, the Chelsea bank offered no chance of getting the three of them to safety but, past the police boat, he could see, emerging through the fog, the huge, rectangular, windowless mass of a building—Nine Elms Cold Store—with a wooden pier beneath it, thrusting out into the river. Nearer, was a larger jetty, partly obscured by a number of barges, sheeted up and riding high in the water. Nicos looked around for something, anything, to use as a makeshift rudder or steering oar, but the only thing to hand was a grip, empty now of provisions. From somewhere deep in his memory, he trawled up the recollection of somebody, somewhere, talking about the steering properties of a sea-anchor. Time: 12.40.

The grip was now their only hope. Providing its handles held! Dropping it gently over the side, maintaining a very firm hold on the handles as the water snatched at it, he found that it did, in fact, give him some control over the craft's direction. Sensing that he could only exercise limited control, he decided to aim for the Cold Store pier—the other jetty was too close for him to have any chance of success there. A few seconds later, his plan explained to his sons, he caught sight of a length of wood, floating on the water.

With the strain on his arm and shoulder becoming almost unbearable, he called to John to recover the wood and assist him in steering the boat. Gritting his teeth, he hung on, better able to concentrate now that Carlo had ceased his crying, and managed, with John's help, to get close to the end of the pier.

The speed of the moving craft, their frozen fingers and cramped positions, all combined to defeat them. With the green-slime-covered timbers evading the clutches of their outstretched hands, the craft, dipping and swaying as they made desperate efforts to recover their balance, swept on towards Vauxhall Bridge, where Nicos could just distinguish a man in unusual clothing crouching near the Vauxhall end.

Back at the box again and peering over the back of it, two things caught Johnston's eye—the back plate was secured with a number of round-headed bolts, while an orange cable issued from a hole in the centre to pass over the side of the bridge. The hole, not painted or rusty, was still shiny as if freshly drilled and was not fitted with a grommet or bush. The cable, about a quarter of an inch in diameter, had a shiny orange covering, similar in many respects to detonating cord. Time: 12.50.

Immersed in his intense study of the box, distant screams broke through his concentration to draw his attention once more up-river. To his astonishment, he saw a partly waterlogged inflatable floating with the tide but veering towards a series of vertical wooden structures standing clear of the water some five yards from his bridge. A row of five of them, each consisting of four massive baulks of timber rising in a narrow pyramid, reached out from the river bank, covering an underwater outfall.

Pushing up his visor and straining his eyes through the fog, he could just make out the figure of a man and two children, the man bent double at the rear of the craft apparently dangling something in the water. The larger child appeared to be holding a piece of wood over the side and, apart from the cries, the overlying impression was of silence. He realised that their engine was not working.

Then, farther away, he noticed a police launch moving out from the river bank near Battersea Power Station, its blue lamp flashing dimly through the fog. Even as he watched he could detect her acceleration as she moved downstream, the moustache of her bow wave rising, growing whiter. Looking down again at the inflatable, he saw that it was going to hit one of the wooden pyramids but, even if the occupants managed to leave the craft there was no way ashore. Standing up, he shouted to the police launch, waving his arms in the inflatable's direction.

The menace beside him now pushed to the back of his mind he concentrated on the inflatable and the desperate struggle of its occupants to avoid disaster. A hopeless, sobbing, wailing sound could be heard coming from the younger child, but the others were silent, too engrossed in their struggle for survival to make any noise. Inching painfully across the tide, they brought the inflatable almost within touching reach of the outermost pyramid, where desperation was almost their undoing. Fear spurred the smaller child to make a frantic grab for safety, recklessly tipping the craft and almost falling into the icy water. The older boy's attempt to restrain him caused the craft to tilt and swerve violently but an idiosyncratic eddy brought it, broadside on, against the timbers.

The police launch had made short work of the remaining distance and was now nearing a point below Andrew Johnston's feet. In addition to throttling back to cut down the bow wave, the coxswain was doing everything possible to avoid worsening Nicos's problems, while one of his crew, in a shouted interchange, queried the danger from the suspected bomb. Responding to the queries, Andrew realised that he had become so involved in the incident that he had been shouting encouragement and suggestions for several minutes, but was unable to recall a single sentence. He suddenly became aware of the fact that his gestures and shouting could have been misinterpreted by all those watching him from the vicinity of Vauxhall Cross. Indeed, he could see activity among the police on both sides of the river; however, using violent and graphic signals, he managed to prevent any further movement towards him from either direction. Any distraction to an explosives officer at work can swiftly lead to disaster, and the occupants of the inflatable would no doubt have been astonished to learn that they had put his life, too, at risk, to say nothing of the havoc that would have been caused had the bomb exploded.

He was grateful that the interruption had occurred at a relatively inactive stage in the proceedings, at a time when although concentrating, he was engaged only in the study of a problem, a cerebral exercise carried out while in a relatively comfortable position. How much more potentially hazardous it would have been if the distraction had insinuated itself into his consciousness just at a moment when he was in some tortured position, stretched to the point where a sudden unscripted move could spell disaster. Anyway, luck had been on his side! He was in control of the situation again, but before resuming his examination of the device he wanted to see the end of the little drama below him.

With superb watermanship, the cosxwain had managed to manoeuvre the launch, stern first, into the gap between the pyramids and the bridge. Stern first because it would be easier to take in survivors over that part of the launch, and downstream to prevent the inflatable being swept away, past them all. With one of the crew using a boathook to hold the launch in position against the pyramid, the other PC leaned over the side and succeeded in lifting Carlo on board. The strain on his shoulder finally forced Nicos to release his hold on the grip and clutch wildly and hopelessly at the side of the launch.

John, meanwhile, his frozen misery and stiffness temporarily forgotten, had scrambled agilely into the launch where he now stood shivering, reaction setting in rapidly. Leaving Carlo, the PC turned his attention to Nicos whose immediate reaction was to envelop him in the drowning man's grip, the vicelike hold which induces its own counter force. Years in the police had been a valuable training ground, and the constable, hunched dangerously over the side of the launch, applied a few dark, secret holds and Nicos, relaxing, was in the launch without conscious effort.

A rope was quickly attached to the inflatable and, opening the throttle, the coxswain steered the launch out of danger, swinging to port and heading back upstream. Nicos and the boys were already forward in the cabin, wrapped in blankets, and a kettle of water was boiling for the preparation of hot drinks. A blast on the launch's siren bade farewell and good luck to Andrew Johnston. Time: 13.05.

Eleven

'God, it's cold enough to freeze the goolies of a brass pawnbroker. Much more of this and I won't be able to react quickly enough to do anything. It's time they spelled us!'

With his attention still firmly centred on the windows of the flat opposite, the speaker eased his cramped muscles, carefully stretching his stiffening limbs and flexing his frozen fingers, unprotected by the woollen mittens. Sluggish circulation was no great asset to a man poised to fire at a difficult target, fleetingly presented.

His colleague showed a deceptive lack of sympathy. 'I'm not surprised! You bloody matelots are all the same. Sitting in your nice warm boats you get soft. All that rum and chef's specials can't be good for you!'

'Sod off, you crazy pongo! And they're ships not boats.'

The radio at their side clicked, putting an end to the argument, but no speech followed. Somebody, accidentally or otherwise, had pressed the transmit button and released it.

Marksmen, members of the élite team of firearms instructors, the two officers were part of a carefully positioned ring of experts whose task, if ordered, would be to take out McAllister. In addition to a hand gun, each was armed with a heavier weapon of his own preference.

The silence on the street below was rent by the sound of a Caribbean voice raised in hysterical anger. Washington Leroy had arrived and, panic-stricken with fear for his family, was a complication that the police could have done without.

Leroy was ethnically a Jamaican, but he sounded like a Cockney, and in reality fell into a nationality gap. Nearly thirty-two years old, he had come into the world in a squalid shanty-town slum outside Kingston but, before he was four years old, the London Transport recruiting campaign had tempted his father to wrench up the family roots in search of a living wage. Twenty months of hard saving and subsistence-level existence had enabled him to bring his wife and three sons to the promised land. Eighteen years later, disillusioned, mother and father had taken an opportunity to return to their Caribbean island, leaving Washington and his two brothers to fend for themselves. After a period of alternating enforced idleness and short-term employment, Washington and his brothers now worked as dustmen.

When the message concerning Janice and his children had been delivered at Sanitation Department offices, Leroy had been out with his team, collecting refuse near the edge of the borough, so it had taken the constable some time to locate him and bring him back. A number of people were beginning to wish that he hadn't. Not the most well-balanced of personalities at the best of times, he had arrived at the stage where any opposition or failure to understand him only made him more unstable. The chip on his shoulder was all too firmly in position.

Rising up from the street through the icy fog, the sound of the altercation insinuated itself through the window where the familiarity of Washington's strident tones registered with Janice's subconscious. Giving no thought to the consequences, she rose from her seat to rush forward to the window.

Aroused abruptly from his private world, McAllister shot forward amidst the screams of the terror-stricken children, grabbed her by the arm and flung her, spinning, to crash against the wall opposite the window. With all the breath knocked out of her, her shoulder numbed by the impact, she subsided in a defenceless heap, the sound of her long, retching sobs pushing back the silence—a silence from the gunman born of the sheer inarticulate, mind-blowing rage of a man balanced on the edge of fatal, unpredictable insanity.

The drama at the window having been observed by the

marksmen, its details were already being transmitted to incident control and the senior police officer. Washington Leroy, unaware of the desperate action in his flat, was being shunted expertly out of earshot, where any reaction from him would not be a distraction.

'What the bloody hell was that all about?' asked one of the marksmen. 'He just went berserk!'

'Buggered if I know. It was all over in a flash.'

'Yes, he never showed more than an arm and a shoulder. There was no bloody chance of getting a shot in even if you were already lined up.'

'Yeah! We're going to need more than that. Some bugger's got to kid him. And I don't see anybody talking him out. Not with a woman and two kids in there. I wonder if they've found out who he is?'

'He's some Jock, supposed to be in the Provisionals. That's all I know.'

'Yeah, but if they can get his name we might be able to find out something worthwhile. It might help to work out what he's likely to do.'

The telephone bell rang hesitantly (field telephones had to be cranked up), but the noise was sufficient to bring McAllister spinning around, with the hair on the back of his neck prickling like a cockatoo's display. Making a desperate effort to regain his self-control he moved across the room to pick up the handset.

A carefully controlled, sober voice asked, 'Who is that, please?'

Kneeling down on the bridge once more, Andrew Johnston resumed his study of the counter box. When this examination was completed, he climbed over the the railing and, clinging to it, hung out over the river in an attempt to see the lower end of the orange cable. Failing to see anything worthwhile, he returned to the pavement and retraced his steps towards Vauxhall.

Once again he was turning over a number of considerations in his mind. . . . *Possibly a pressure system linked to the rubber tube . . . Delayed arming probable . . . Could be a mercury anti-tilt switch in the box, or anti-lift—or both . . . perhaps an anti-removal switch on the back plate . . . Is it detonating cord? Or is it a cable—and the device booby-trapped? . . . Underneath—under the bridge—could there be an anti-removal trap? . . . What type seems most likely? . . .*

Without doubt, he had to bring two things back with him—the special cutting gear (he must get a hole in the casing of the box) and a hook ladder from the fire brigade (to go over the side of the bridge).

Aboard the police launch, now back on station at Battersea, the coxswain was making his views known. 'Mr Georgiou, what possessed you to go on the river in a craft like that in weather like this? You're lucky to be alive!'

'I had made promise to my boys long time ago. They not have long holiday. Breaking promises is not good, I think.'

'But surely you could see the weather! It must have been bad when you left Mortlake. In any case you haven't got the right clothes on to be out in these conditions. And the boat isn't good enough—it's too old, the canvas is worn, you've got no pump and the engine's useless. I wouldn't go out on the Serpentine the way you've been on the river today! And where are your life jackets?'

'I am not rich man—I cannot afford better boat. The man who sold it said everything OK. I do not know about boats. Why life jacket? Is only a river.'

'Today you ran another risk, Mr Georgiou, a risk that you could not even have known about. That man on the bridge, the one in the unusual gear, he is an explosives officer and he was trying to deal with a bomb. If we had not caught you when we did you might well have made him set off the bomb by mistake! And it's a big bomb, big enough to have killed you and both your sons. After all, you had no means of controlling the time that you arrived at the bridge, you had no control over your dinghy, and you might have been right underneath him when he was trying to do something dangerous—something requiring all his attention.'

'How was I to know? I only trying to give my boys a treat on the river.'

'What a bloody fool!' said one of the constables later. 'Here we are with all the traffic stopped, no lighters, no colliers, nothing moving at all, and this bloke comes blundering through. Shouldn't have been allowed out without a minder. What sort of bloke is he anyway? Sounded Italian to me.'

'Well,' said the coxswain, 'he's not. He's a Greek Cypriot. The poor sod's had a hard time. They don't all end up driving Mercs and running brothels.'

'Yeah, but what I can't forgive is bringing them two kids,' said the other PC. 'Neither of them could swim and they were frozen through. There's no way he could have saved them in these conditions. We could have been out later, trying to find the bodies. It's bad enough with grown-ups but it turns me over when we have to fish for youngsters.'

'He's just a mug,' said the coxswain, 'a mug with no money trying to look after his kids. You take your kids out, don't you? But you're right—he's a bloody fool, and I told him as much. That commotion can't have helped the chap on the bridge either—I think he was in the middle of doing something tricky. Interruptions like that must take some swallowing—you wouldn't wonder if he lost his bottle! And he's still got to finish off. He's been at it a long time already.'

'Yeah,' said the second PC. 'He can have his job for me. Those blokes earn every penny they get! Incidentally, sarge, what are we going to do with the dinghy?'

'I told the father we'd get it back to Barnes. He can pick it up there later. But it won't be today. I might be able to get one of our chaps to have a look at the outboard. Personally, I don't think any of it's worth salvaging.'

Behind the steamed-up windows, the cheap café and sandwich bar in the Strand was deliciously warm and redolent of the smells of food and hot drinks, a haven of luxurious peace in sharp contrast to the misery of the street outside. Shuffling past the display cabinets on top of the counter, bearing the shepherd's pie and tea that they had selected, the two girls stopped at the cash register to hand over their luncheon vouchers, then passed on to sit at one of the tables.

'They're saying in our office that Waterloo Station is closed and there aren't no trains running.'

'It's true, Linda. I heard it on the radio. One of our typists has got a trannie in the office. There's a bomb at Vauxhall and the trains have all stopped. They didn't say how long for. I hope it's finished in time for us to get home OK.'

'Yes, Sue, I hope so too. If it's still closed there'll be an awful muck-up. You can get home on the tube but I'll have to try my luck on a bus. They're sure to be full up. Anyway, I expect a lot of them won't run in the fog.'

'The tubes will be packed too, you can bet, and all those gropers will be having a field day. What say, Linda, if Waterloo is still closed, we get something to eat and then have a night out? Go to the pictures or something. Have you got enough money?'

'I might have but if I haven't I can borrow some. Why don't you give me a ring later? About half-past three.'

Setting about the shepherd's pie they carried on chattering like a pair of sparrows.

Andrew Johnston left the pedestrian tunnel, passed quickly through the station tunnel area and found the police group standing out on the pavement. He lost no time in sketching in the situation on the bridge as he saw it, together with a graphic summary of the river rescue plus the odd comment on the stupidity of people who did such things without preparation.

'Those River chaps did a fantastic job—without them we'd have had three dead. If somebody wants to do something I'm perfectly willing to write a statement—the coxswain deserves recognition of some sort. He was magnificent—a bloody professional.'

Clem Jones had come up to the group, so Andrew asked him about the cutting gear and, getting a satisfactory answer—it was stowed and ready in the Transit—invited him to borrow a hook ladder from the fire brigade. Also to check if there was any rope available.

Turning back to the police group, he asked where the civilian representatives had gone and was told that they had all repaired to a local pub to continue their discussion in more congenial surroundings. 'How sensible!' he commented.

Then Pat Warlock, who had been radiating increasing impatience, broke in. 'What are you going to do now? It seems to me this job's starting to drag and the whole area is still tied up. Outside pressures are growing and I've got to satisfy the ACC about progress. I'd also like to give the media something—they're getting to be very stroppy. They may well do something silly if we don't let them loose.'

'Well, I've got a different set of priorities. I'm also concerned about progress, only I'm not playing politics. The sooner I get this lot finished the earlier I can get back and join all the desk drivers at the Yard. You know my views on the media—we've talked about it before on a number of occasions. I know they have got a job to do but not to the detriment of my safety. No way! The best of them are absolutely trustworthy but there's some right bloody pirates among them—and we've had one already! You must excuse my bluntness but I'm damned near frozen through, I'm bloody hungry, I haven't had a drink for hours and I *have* been working on my priority—keeping me alive. I haven't been swanning around wondering which side is my best for the camera. I've had a good look at the box, but there's more to do before I can work on the next move. It's absolutely essential that I get a look inside it, and also underneath the bridge. Once that's done we can make the final decisions, agree priorities and then get on with the real work—clearing the devices.'

'Sure, Major. I do appreciate your problems, believe me.

I'll go back to Pendennis and try to calm them down. Give them some load of fanny. I'll be back in half an hour—will you be finished by then?'

'Could be. I'll try. You can bet that I won't take any longer than necessary. It's freezing out there, you know.'

Clem Jones had now returned triumphantly with the hook ladder and a length of one and half inch hemp. His 'boot-neck' skills were still alive.

'Stick them in the Transit, please, Clem. Leave Wheelbarrow where it is. I shan't be using it on the bridge. Did you check the generator? There's no way that I can carry all the gear up the bridge and it's still a one-man job at this stage. So I'll drive the Transit myself.'

To Peter Barwell, he said, 'I'm afraid the chaps in the lorry park office will have to move—that office will be no protection at all if there's an explosion from the bridge. In fact it could easily make matters worse. They're too near. Find them somewhere else, please, Peter. And ask MP Mobile to get in touch with my office. Tell them to ring the Explosives Liaison Officer at Woolwich—I want him to bring up a powder wagon for the explosive. Thanks.' Time: 13.38.

Climbing into the Transit, he switched on and drove off, making a U-turn, then out into the open through Kennington Road arch. Weaving through the islands he drove quickly on to Bridgefoot, then climbed up the slope towards the box, stopping about ten yards short of the rubber tube. It was hardly the time to set anything off by being careless or not paying attention. After unloading the cutting gear, he ran out a cable from the generator which he had already started running, and positioned the cutter conveniently near the counter box.

He settled himself comfortably, struck the cutter flame and brought it near to the top of the box, carefully avoiding any contact with it, then started to cut a circular hole about two inches in diameter, making small systematic adjustments to produce the optimum cutting rate. The prime advantage of this cutter was its short flame and the rapid heat dissipation within the target, making unlikely an accidental ignition of the contents. Stopping with about half an inch to go, Andrew Johnston put down the cutter and, rising warily to his feet, stretched himself deliciously against the stiffness bred and nourished by the biting cold.

Reaching into the pocket where he had pouched a roll of strong impact adhesive tape, he took it out and cut off a length of about two feet. He wrapped one end around his left hand and bared two inches of the adhesive surface at the other end, then, fishing delicately, he managed to get it to adhere to the centre of the almost completed circle.

Tapping it very gently with the end of the middle finger of his right hand, he settled the tape more firmly, conscious all the time of the vital need to avoid any movement of the box. Picking up the cutting head again, he traced out the final cut, releasing the circle of metal, which he very carefully lifted clear on the end of the tape and placed on the ground.

He stood up once more, moved over to the cutting gear control unit, switched it off, and returned the head to its clip. Back at the Transit he shut down the generator, then took out the hook ladder and rope to lay them on the pavement against the railings, ready for the stage after next.

Crouching again, a bit more creakily this time—cold and the long hours were getting at him—he looked through the hole and was startled almost out of his skin. As he had tilted his head forward, his visor, not properly secured, had slid down in front of his startled eyes. The expression that he used was succinct, explosive and deeply satisfying. It was little incidents, slips, like that that caused disasters.

With his visor pushed back again, firmly this time, and secured, he shone his torch into the hole. A glow of satisfaction spread up from his gut—the feeling of 'I told you so' in the most gratifying circumstances—as the mechanism was exposed with all suggested variables present and available: the arming clock, the pressure contact wires leading from the rubber tube, two mercury switches at right angles, one on the back plate, and an Ever Ready battery, a 4½ volt No. 124.

Amidst the small maze of coloured wires completing the internal circuits he could see the ultimate prize, his gold cup, the jackpot. Two instantaneous detonators, connected in parallel, were taped to the orange cable, a short distance from its sealed-up end. Only it wasn't a cable—it was detonating cord after all. With a tiny sense of anti-climax, he pulled in some of the orange slack, taped it to the railings and cut it carefully, just outside the box, separating the two ends and taping them down.

Yet again, the chill knifing through his clothes reached the film of sweat and he was engulfed in a convulsive shiver travelling all the way up from his knees. Glancing involuntarily back towards the railway, he could just see a bundle lying on the pavement, close in against the wall at the far end of the Kennington Road tunnel. The white helmet gave it away—it was Clem Jones covering him with the 'scope, good old Clem, the 'bootneck', backing him—he was alone no longer, though come to that he never had been. He made a flamboyant thumbs-up sign and Clem waved his acknowledgement, then turned to speak to somebody concealed behind him. The success was known back there now. Time: 13.57.

Picking up the hook ladder, he passed it over the side, seating it firmly on top of the railing, keeping clear of the box which was still a hazard, and lashed it firmly in place with one end of the rope. Forming the other end into a bowline he stepped into it, feeding the loop up over his hips until it settled under his armpits, securing the running part of the rope behind the press-studs of the top left-hand pocket of his weatherproof. Paying out sufficient rope, he knotted it firmly, very firmly, to the railings. He was not, repeat not, going down that ladder without a safety line. He didn't want to go down anyway but, if he had to, and he had to, then a safety line, as far as he was concerned, was a must.

Climbing carefully over the side of the bridge, he set his foot gingerly on the ladder, speculatively testing it for stability while retaining a firm grip on the railing. Then, settling his safety line to prevent any chance of entanglement, he went slowly down the ladder, the road surface rising in jerks up to, then above, his eye level. When he reached the working position he found that, by a piece of good fortune, he had placed the ladder so that the bundle lay just to his right, his working hand. He pressed himself against the rungs to study the layout. In his time he had moulded himself against warmer and softer objects and survived!

Twelve

'Sean McAllister,' he replied, thrown completely off balance by the unexpected question.

A long silence followed as the negotiator savoured the astonishing success of his totally off-the-cuff stratagem. As he cranked the calling handle his attention had been nothing more than a simple opening query. Just to get the show on the road.

'Hello, Mr McAllister. My name is Youngman, Stephen Youngman. Is everybody all right in there?'

'What do you want to know for?'

'Well, we heard some noise and are wondering what happened.'

'The stupid bitch didn't do as she was told. I told her to sit still and she moved to the window. It was her own bloody fault.'

Youngman, Detective Superintendent and qualified negotiator, allowed the lull to develop. Now that he had made contact his main concern was to cool everything down, then gradually, quietly, gain control to the point where rational discussion could take place. Patience was going to be his most important weapon.

'McAllister, do you need anything to eat? Anything to drink? Anything to smoke? I might be able to help with something in that line.'

'A bottle of whisky and some cigars. Nothing else.'

'I really meant something like tea or coffee. Something hot. Soup even. Surely Mrs Leroy and her children would like something. It must be very cold in there.'

'Whisky and cigars. Nothing else!'

'I don't know about the whisky, Mr McAllister. I'll have to ask the man in charge. I can get the cigars, but it will take a little while.'

'Get good ones, not those stupid little whiffs. Who do you have to ask about the whisky? I thought you were in charge.'

'He's the man I work for. Mr McAllister, will you let Mrs Leroy and her children come out? They must be very frightened, and keeping them in there won't do you any good in the end.'

'Sod off, you Sassenach bastard! You get me that whisky and those cigars. And next time I want to speak to the man in charge, the high head yin. Not you!'

A firm click in the earphone told Youngman that the conversation had ended. There was no way that he could tell whether the handset had been slammed down on the cradle or not—the sound would be the same. But McAllister had sounded as if he was getting tensed up again. This was going to take a long time.

Settled securely on the ladder with his left arm firmly locked around it, Andrew Johnston was concentrating his attention on the point where the detonating cord, having led over the bulge, disappeared under the bridge. From now on, each step forward had to be preceded by careful study of the situation and all the options.

Concentrating even more closely because of the difficulty, in the poor light, of trying to follow the orange cord against the orange paint of the bridge, he gradually became conscious of something throbbing. Perhaps because his close-fitting helmet had been designed to muffle sound, the sensation was felt rather than heard. Its growing insistence, gradually changing towards audibility, penetrated his awareness, demanding his attention.

The first mystery—how that noise could be coming from the bomb—passed little by little to a conviction that there was no way that the bomb could be involved. Suddenly, like a physical impact, it dawned upon him that the noise was behind him, coming through his shoulder blades. His binoral sense, dulled by concentration, had played him false and was 180 degrees out. Time: 14.07.

As he swung round in the direction of the sound, still with no idea of the source, he almost lost his grip on the ladder, but, swaying violently, heart in mouth, he managed to regain stability. The throbbing had now increased to a roar with heavy fluttering, swishing overtones—the hallmark of the helicopter. Comprehension dawned—the media had lost its patience, the thirst for news was becoming a massive craving on a par with drug addiction, undiminished, even heightened, by danger.

Steady now in his perch on the ladder he relieved his feelings by shaking his fist at the figures in the cabin. The passenger on the left, completely oblivious to any danger that they were creating, was pointing a cine-camera with a telescopic lens through the door. Relieving his pent-up feelings even more by shouting obscenities against the ear-splitting, enveloping sound, he waved them savagely away, but the aircraft clattered past near enough to buffet him with its down-draught. It lifted over him, over the lorry park, to survey the situation at Vauxhall Cross, then, arrogantly, impudently, returned to the river to hover for fully two minutes, drinking its fill, before finally throwing up its head and cantering back through the fog to Westland Heliport.

'I hope the bastards land in the sodding mud,' he said aloud. 'I'll have something to say when I see that bloody Warlock! They're not going to get away with that, the selfish bastards.'

Dismissing the thought that he might climb back on the bridge, he turned his attention back to the bundle and deliberately relaxed his muscles, stretching each leg in turn while regaining his composure. This was certainly not the time to take chances or make foolish errors, or even be attacked by cramp.

The bundle, enveloped in a black plastic dustbin bag was

jammed into one of the smaller spaces between the white vertical girders, filling practically all the available space, the detonating cord disappearing into the small gap in the top corner. It was almost certain that there was no secondary timing circuit. Setting up a situation like this in the dark would not have allowed of any frills. It would have been either anti-removal or nothing. That meant that this problem could be left until later. The car was now definitely the priority job.

The fog was thickening again, he was getting stiffer and colder, and he could do with a break and some refreshment. He'd been out in the open for a long time, and standing on a ladder was more tiring than people realised. Climbing wearily back up the ladder back on to the pavement, he looked towards Clem Jones, miming the actions of eating and drinking. When Clem waved 'message received and understood', he stepped out of the rope loop, left the cutting gear where it was, disconnected the cable from the generator and climbed into the Transit. Starting up, he drove back to the Lambeth Road control point. Time: 14.43.

After prayers, business in the House of Commons opened at 14.48, the House having sat with due ceremony at 14.30. Sparsely attended, with much of the green leather visible, there was a growing air of expectation nevertheless that a statement would be made later regarding the terrorist situation.

Stephen Youngman wound the calling handle vigorously, then waited. Still no response. He had been trying to raise McAllister for a good fifteen minutes without success, but patience was the name of his game. He rang again, and sat with the earpiece pressed closely to his ear.

'What do you want now?' McAllister asked.

'I've got you some cigars, but my guv'nor says you can't have the whisky. The cigars are in the bag ready to come down to you. Is there anything else you want?'

'If I can't have the whisky you can stick the bloody cigars up your arse. Where's the head man anyway? I told you before, I'm not talking to you!'

'He's not here at the moment, so I'm afraid that you'll *have* to talk to me. I'll leave the cigars in the bag outside your window so you can take them in when you like.'

'They can stay there and bloody well rot. I don't want them.'

'Well, Mr McAllister, that's up to you. How are Mrs Leroy and the children? Are they all right?'

'They're keeping quiet. They know what's good for them!'

'Mr McAllister, can we talk about you letting them come out? They can't be doing any good in there and we can bring them out without any danger to you.'

The discussion flowed back and forth, haltingly at first, but Youngman's patience and persistence were gradually producing an increasing element of calmness in the gunman.

Inside the flat, Janice was watching McAllister as he sat talking into the telephone. She could sense the tension subsiding, and rose gingerly to her feet intending to go into the kitchen to get a drink for her children. His attention drawn back to her, McAllister broke off his conversation to demand an explanation. Grudgingly accepting her answer, he put the telephone to his ear again with a dismissive wave of his hand in her direction.

Reappearing a little later from the kitchen, a patent feeder in one hand and a Bugs Bunny mug in the other, she caught sight of the carrier bag hanging outside the window. Giving the drinks to her children, she asked, 'Shall I get that in for you?'

'Leave the bloody thing alone!' McAllister snapped.

'But what's in it? Do you know?'

'It's some cigars and I don't want them. They might have done something to them. You can't trust any of the bastards.'

Outside, the grimy figure of Washington Leroy broke free

of cover to stand in the centre of the road, looking up at the bag hanging outside the open window of his flat. The continuing efforts to sooth and distract him had been counter-productive. He wasn't going to believe what any copper said, least of all a white one. They were all prejudiced against him and his fellow immigrants.

Overlying the suspicion was his blind fear for Janice and the kids, gnawing at his guts to the threshold of physical sickness. Unattended for a short period, he took the opportunity to slip away and out through the cordon into the street. There, consumed with helplessness, eaten up with a feeling of impotence and unable to understand why nobody had taken the bag inside, he took refuge in noise. Raising his voice, he shouted, 'Hey, man! You in there! Why you keeping my family locked up, man? They done nothing to you. What kind of man, you? Some sort of crazy man?'

The sound of his voice brought responses on two levels. Two constables started forward from behind cover in the street, one with drawn revolver, intending to grab him and pull him down into shelter. In the flat, McAllister's slowly developing composure was irretrievably broken by that voice. For all Washington Leroy's long sojourn in London, stress was liable to bring out the Jamaican sing-song delivery of his formative years, and the accent triggered off McAllister's pathological detestation of anything to do with non-whites, which transcended even his blind hatred of the English. He gave vent to his fury, throwing down the handset and lunging towards the window, automatic in hand. Janice was brushed violently aside on the way, ending up, once more, semi-conscious on the floor.

All thoughts of caution driven out, McAllister appeared at the window to snatch off two shots in rapid succession at the target of his unreasoning fury standing in the middle of the road. Failing, in his mindless rage, to compensate fully for the pull of his powerful weapon, the first shot smashed into Leroy's left shoulder, spinning him violently away from the second bullet which, screaming off the road surface, splintered a window behind him.

Still standing at the window, McAllister turned, pointing the gun at the little boy. His finger tightened on the trigger.

Thirteen

Parking the Transit next to the canteen wagon which now stood against the kerb with its rear doors open, scenting the air with the delicious aromas of piping hot pies and coffee, Andrew Johnston opened one rear door of his van and wearily collapsed on to the seat offered by the edge of the vehicle, gratefully accepting the coffee and pie that Clem had produced and attacking them with vigour. He now realised just how cold he was, and his stomach told him how welcome another of those pies would be.

As Clem went for the replenishment, Warlock came up. Andrew directed a belligerent stare at him. 'That last pantomime was bloody criminal! You couldn't see in Pendennis, but I was on the ladder just about to start a close examination of the stuff under the bridge, and then that bloody lunatic in the chopper appeared! I just couldn't believe that anybody could be so damned stupid. It must have taken some time to organise! You can't hire a helicopter on impulse. You don't pick one up like a flounder with its flag up! If that's where Force policy is leading us—they can stuff it! There was a time when the only TV copper was Dixon of Dock Green. Now you're all carrying Equity cards. I'd like to meet the buffoon in the chopper, but I suppose that it would be just as well if I didn't! Anyway, Pat, I'm finished on the subject for now, but I'm still bloody angry, and I shall be putting it on paper later!'

'Yes, I understand. But it would help if you could fill us in on the details of how the job is going so that I can feed the lions. They're starving, and until I can give them a few crumbs, it's difficult to stop them breaking out of the cage.

Besides, someone's got to give them a bit of a rocket—there's the helicopter business, and that chap on the roof of Camelford House, and now we've got more trouble. You know Rivermill House, that block of flats at the other end of Vauxhall Bridge? Well, one of the nationals has got a man into a flat near the top, with a telephoto camera.'

'Oh, no!' Andrew said.

'I expect we'll be able to put a stop to it, but we'll need something to sugar the pill in the way of solid information.'

'All right.'

'Thanks. The overseas press is beginning to get interested as well. And,' Warlock continued, preening a little, 'I've been asked to do a bit for TV. Both channels want something for the news.'

'Bully for you,' remarked Andrew drily. He suggested that, with the risk from the bridge minimised, they should all move back into the station tunnel for his briefing, and when the group had reassembled, he described in detail his actions on the bridge and under it, not forgetting the incidents involving Nicos Georgiou and the helicopter. Bert Smith looked thunderous as the Explosives Officer spoke of how easily such distractions could lead to disaster—if he had anything to do with it, somebody was going to suffer!

'So, gentlemen,' Johnston went on, 'the position up there is this. Except for two detonators and a short length of detonating cord, the counter box is clear and quite safe, unless somebody touches it.'

'But we can't open the bridge or the river, can we?' broke in Warlock.

'We can't anyway, with the car not cleared. Until that bastard is dealt with everything is at a standstill. Which leads me to my next point. The car timer and any mercury switch, in my opinion, were in the box that I took out of circuit when I shot away the leads, so, in practical terms, that leaves the possibility of an anti-withdrawal system, or an anti-movement switch. There could be another timer, hidden away this time, but I don't believe there is. Nevertheless, I'm not prepared to move the car—any alternative location is just as bad and, at least, there's no danger of snipers where it is now. So I propose to deal with thc car first, then the bridge, and the railway people can get on with the preliminaries for getting the trains started in about an hour.'

'Incidentally, Major,' Peter Barwell asked, 'what would happen if the one under the river bridge went up?'

'Total bloody disaster! A bloody big hole in the road and the girders underneath chewed up to hell. The abutment well wrecked. The whole of that span could collapse into the river. Quite a lot of blast damage around too.'

As the group was breaking up, thinking deeply about that sobering opinion, another figure entered the tunnel. It was Bomb Seven, Frank Norrie. Andrew Johnston advanced to meet him, 'What the hell are you doing here, Frank? I thought that you had several jobs of your own to keep you occupied?'

'I've come to see if you've finished with Wheelbarrow—it's the only one available at the moment and I could use it. Also, I thought that it would be worth having a look to see if you want any help.'

'You're welcome to Wheelbarrow, Frank. It's time to do the job properly and earn the money.' He noticed Frank's scoffing look, and went on, 'What are you grinning about? I know it's an unfashionable attitude, particularly among the inexperienced, but I've never liked working with robots—there's nothing to beat your own eyes and ears and fingers.'

'You don't have to tell me, Andy—I'm with you all the way. But there are times when I'd rather it was Wheelbarrow that gets blown to bits than me.'

'Yes, it has its uses. I was glad to have it here at the beginning of this car job, but I've finished with it now. If you need the cutter you'll have to wait until it's back in the van. Thanks all the same, but I don't need any help. There's not too much to do anyway.'

Turning back to Warlock, he said, 'Once I've cleared the car I think it'll be OK to bring the media down. We can organise a place for them to photograph it from and they can also get some shots of the bridge with the counter box. That should get them off your back—there won't be many left after they've taken their happy snaps. Fifteen minutes should cover it and I'll keep out of the way while it's going on. Then you can get on with your magic lantern bit.'

Warlock nodded grimly, just succeeding in controlling his temper. Before he could say anything, Bert Smith came up. 'You feeling all right, Andy?'

'Just about. Is that canteen wagon still here? I could do with another pie before I get started.'

The third shot rang out, echoing off the walls of the buildings almost before Washington Leroy had slumped to the ground. McAllister sprawled inelegantly, lifeless, on the floor of the flat. In spite of the distraction of Leroy's dramatic appearance in the street, the marksman's patient concentration had ended the siege.

In the street a frozen tableau showed the armed policeman at the crouch, his revolver aimed, two-handed, at the window, and his colleague halted in mid-flight just short of Leroy's prostrate figure. In the flat, the children's piercing screams of fear obliterated the tinny sound of Stephen Youngman's voice emerging from the dangling handset, as he tried desperately to find out what was happening. His job as a negotiator was over. Time: 14.52.

The disruption of central London has continued to pose serious problems to road and rail traffic. Two different sections of Irish terrorism, the Provisional IRA and the INLA have claimed responsibility for a number of incidents. Traffic is still at a standstill in the Vauxhall Cross area and there have been no trains in or out of Waterloo Station for over five hours. Two large bombs have been found in the area and are being dealt with . . . During the day other incidents have occurred at Holborn and Oxford Street, but have been satisfactorily cleared . . . There is a further report of a bomb being found in Shaftesbury Avenue, and this is being investigated . . . Another report is just coming in that the hostage situation in Islington has been resolved. Further details will be given when they become available . . . The condition of the explosives expert who was seriously injured in Greenwich early this morning is now giving rise to concern . . . A statement on today's incidents will be made in the House of Commons this evening by the Home Secretary . . .

The electric kettle's automatic switch clicked out, isolating the power supply just as the vapour from the spout was developing into a thickening plume. The steam's sense of disappointment was almost tangible as Jean Johnston disconnected the cord from the rear of the kettle and poured boiling water into the green Berylware teapot standing on the nearby worktop. Waiting for the tea to draw, she wondered whether Andrew would be home on time or whether they were at the start of yet another period of uncertainty.

That had been the pattern all those years ago when he set up the section, clearing job after job, doing his own driving, with only the periodic telephone call from widely separated locations to suggest some theoretical home-coming time, which rarely turned out to be accurate. As the unit had grown, with more officers to share the work, life had become a little easier, but Andrew could never be sure when he would be free and that made it difficult to plan their social engagements. To buy theatre tickets in advance or to invite friends to dinner sometimes seemed to be a direct invitation to the gods to devise some incident which would prevent Andrew from getting home before the evening was over.

Of course it was part of the job, and she had got used to it in time, but if these bomb attacks intensified it would be as bad as the early days again, and that didn't bear thinking about.

She poured tea into two cups and took them through to the breakfast room where her elderly aunt was seated in her favourite chair, chewing the print off the morning paper.

Apart from a break for lunch, they had talked and knitted their way through several hours, pausing from time to time to listen or look at the news broadcasts. She had barely placed her bottom on the chair when the telephone bell sounded its imperious double notes from the other end of the hall. Walking quickly and apprehensively to the telephone she picked it up to hear Clem Jones forecasting Andrew's late, as yet unpredictable, return. While Andrew had been enjoying the well-earned hot pies, Clem had phoned his own wife to put her in the picture and had then decided to ring Jean. Having given her a brief account of the day's events so far, he promised to phone again later.

It took a long time for Jean's stomach to stop churning over with fear of the unknown, the dreadful anticipation set in motion by the sound of the telephone bell.

Back in the breakfast room, she commented, 'Andrew is still dealing with something at Vauxhall. I don't know what it is but Clem Jones says they think he's done the worst bit. And there's two to deal with. So I won't make any plans for his food. We'll have ours at the normal time. Oh, blast! We've missed the three o'clock news. I must listen to the four o'clock. There ought to be something worthwhile on then.'

Fourteen

The Pendennis House conference room was not a happy place, the bedlam of multi-national sound being shrouded in a swirling fog of poisonous tobacco smoke. It was clearer outside or, at least, it had been twenty minutes before! Small tables and chairs had been rushed in to give some semblance of a press facility while, along one wall, a few hastily installed telephones had narrowly averted a riot.

The press, still up-tight, was otherwise relaxing, ties loosened, jackets discarded, sleeves rolled up, handbags slung over chairbacks or on the floor. Cigarette ends littered the floor as well as filling the limited number of ashtrays to overflowing and the partly-filled metal waste-paper bins were each surrounded by a scattering of badly aimed litter—empty cigarette packets, crumpled paper, screwed-up tissues and fired matchbooks.

An expanding pool of anticipatory silence spread out from the door which had opened to admit Warlock, Macleod and Gregory. They advanced to the head of the room, the last few steps in a silence broken only by two rather uncomplimentary but perceptive comments, one American and one Glaswegian.

Pat Warlock, flushed and obviously upset by the remarks, opened the batting. 'Ladies and gentlemen, I must apologise for not returning at 12.30 as I said I would, but a number of advances have been made in the three hours since I last spoke to you and we are going to bring you up to date, as far as we can. The Explosives Officer pushed on with the investigation of the car bomb to the stage where he felt that the immediate danger had disappeared. Then a second device was found on Vauxhall Bridge——'

Dwight Hoffman of the Washington *Globe* interrupted. 'How did he deal with the car, Commander? Did he remote it? And has he got a name?'

'I'm afraid I'm not at liberty to answer either point. To continue, this second device had to be checked out before carrying on with the car, so he diverted his efforts to that and found that, while part of the bomb is on the pavement, there is also a large charge of explosive under the bridge.'

Hoffman, who had had some success with his pushy, caustic style in Northern Ireland where he had acquired a superficial knowledge of the subject, broke in again. 'My readers throughout the United States expect me to get these details, Commander. When will I be able to interview your Explosives Officer?'

'Mr Hoffman, is it? Well, I doubt very much if you will. We have quite definite rules over here about that. For their safety, of course.'

Tom Gravell of the London *Daily Signal*, a burly, greying man, well-known and respected, said, 'I believe that he had a couple of outside difficulties, Pat, as well as having to deal with the bomb?'

'Yes, Tom, but I think our Press Department chaps will be dealing with those later. Anyway, the Explosives Officer has cleared the part of the bomb on the pavement and is happy to leave the rest until later—at least, that is what he tells me. The position now is that he has decided to clear the car first, and I have agreed. This will enable the railways to start running again. If he hasn't already started, ladies and gentlemen, he will shortly be dealing with the car and as soon as he has finished, you will be told.'

'When can we get some footage, Pat? When can we get near the scene?' This came from Brian Morton, a television news reporter who was understandably unhappy with the poor quality of the picture he could get in this room with its excessively smoky atmosphere.

'It has been decided that you will be given facilities after the car has been completely cleared and before he starts on the bridge. We'll do our best for you but you must realise that we must be concerned, as always, for your safety.'

This last remark was received with a somewhat bemused silence, few of those present being certain whether to take it at face value or to suspect the usually bland Commander Warlock of an uncharacteristic irony. It was not long, however, before the room was once more filled with sound as each reporter tried to put his questions. Warlock dealt with them skilfully, pacifying whose who were hostile, replying patiently when he was repeatedly asked about matters which he had already covered, keeping a good-natured, smiling composure at all times.

Macleod listened with grudging admiration. He was no fonder of Warlock than was Andrew Johnston, and he was not sure either whether he approved of this new policy of full co-operation with the news-hounds, but he had to admit that Warlock was remarkably adept at projecting the image of a capable, well-briefed officer who recognised the power of the press and would help its members as much as he could. It was obvious that even the most aggressive of the reporters accorded him their respect and many of them gave him their liking too.

After a while, Warlock called for silence. 'I'm sorry, but that must be all for the present, at least from me. I am going now to report to my superiors and to check on the latest position. Meanwhile, the Press Officer has something to say to you, and I would ask you to pay the closest attention to him. We don't like having to treat you like naughty children, but sometimes we just have to speak frankly.' He temporarily stifled the hum of comment by promising to return later, and left the room.

The buzz of conversation resumed as the Press Officer got to his feet. It had been agreed beforehand that he would take over at this point, and he had been amused by Warlock's eagerness to avoid confrontation with the press. What he had not expected, however, was an introduction which seemed calculated to give him an antagonistic audience. All he could do was to speak from the heart and hope that his sincerity and the importance of his message would get through to them. *Christian, up and smite them*!

'Ladies and gentlemen,' he began, 'it's my unhappy task to bring to your notice a couple of pretty unfriendly actions this afternoon. Believe me, I do have some understanding of what editorial pressures can be, but, when somebody's life is placed unnecessarily, even carelessly, at risk, in any manner, we do have to reconsider the priorities. The first problem is that one of your papers has set up an observation point in a top flat in Rivermill House on the other side of the river. Now, I recognise the argument that, with his helmet and other gear on, people will not be able to put a name to the Explosives Officer, but part of the understanding about not photographing these chaps is to avoid any risk of the way that they work becoming known. I accept the view that this is a borderline case but we all know that you cannot control what happens to film—and we're talking about newsreel here—after you've submitted it. The second item is, however, much more serious. I am told that, while the Explosives Officer was at a particularly critical point in his examination of the explosive under the Bridge, he was buzzed by a chopper taking pictures. What's more, the chopper overflew him, then hung around for several minutes making a hell of a noise. Apart from the fact that the Explosives Officer nearly fell into the river, he was also trying to hear if there was anything ticking. His concentration had already been broken by the incident with the boat and, understandably, he was very angry with this "cowboy" episode—very angry indeed. Another incident was dealt with earlier and involved a photographer on the roof of Camelford House who had got through the security cordon. He was, admittedly, a free-lance, but he could easily have got himself shot and it doesn't make co-operation any easier. Ladies and gentlemen, I do ask you to play the game and be reasonable.'

It seemed to have worked. *Peace shall follow battle.* They sat subdued but not over-resentful.

A final question to Macleod came from Tom Gravell. 'Commander, there's a whisper that today's activities are being raised in the House this afternoon—have you heard anything about it?'

'I believe that this is possible, Tom, but Commander Warlock ought to be able to answer that when he returns. And now, ladies and gentlemen, if there are no further questions, we'll wrap this up. Thank you for being so patient.'

Fiona Hawke stepped from the Hillman Hunter, passing through the door into the hospital reception area, where a WRAC sergeant introduced herself and then led the way to the surgeon's office.

Colonel Yates got up as she entered, moved round from behind his desk and ushered her, for the second time, towards the low table and easy chairs, his attitude this time even more solicitous. The office door opened to admit his secretary, carrying a tray of tea things. At a nod from the Colonel, she settled herself into a third chair.

'Mrs Hawke,' the Colonel said, 'you've already met my secretary, Julia Parsons. I'd like her to stay if you don't mind—apart from her other qualifications she is a qualified and highly competent nurse.'

The tea was dispensed and the plate of biscuits handed round, but this did nothing to dispel the feeling of apprehension that was dangerously near overwhelming Fiona. Sensing her concern, Colonel Yates began the little speech he had prepared. 'Mrs Hawke, in all the years that I have been practising I have never grown accustomed to this situation. One tries to develop a style of doing things and most people are grateful for it, but it can never be easy.'

Fiona sat silently in her chair, her eyes fixed on his face. She sipped at her tea, but as she replaced the cup in the saucer, a slight clatter of sound signalled her tension. The longing for him to stop beating about the bush and come to the point competed with a silent scream pleading that he should stop talking, and tell her nothing more. She could feel nausea taking hold, her palms becoming clammy, and the demand for movement, any movement, was growing, but she remained still and silent, slumping slightly in the chair.

Colonel Yates continued, 'As you know, your husband was in the operating theatre for quite some time. We had a number of things to do—his face, his arm, his leg, and on closer examination we found heavy bruising to his back and a couple of cracked ribs. The blast must have thrown him heavily against something very hard. But all that is more or less routine, and none of those injuries was of a really serious nature. It's the effect on his lungs that is worrying me—that and the heavy shock reaction. I am afraid that your husband is losing ground, and I am hoping that you can reverse that trend.'

Fiona straightened in her chair, making as if to speak, but the surgeon held up his hand before going on: 'I am aware that there have been differences between you and your husband—he has been talking rather a lot in his delirium—but, in my experience, the presence of a wife at the bedside often exerts a calming influence; intangible, but real nevertheless. I appreciate that it won't be comfortable and that it will most likely be tiring but we will do everything to support you.'

'Naturally, I shall do anything that you ask. Of course, I didn't come prepared to stay and there are things that I shall need. Perhaps somebody could arrange for them to be brought here?'

'That's no problem at all, Mrs Hawke. And thank you for agreeing to stay. Mrs Parsons has managed to locate the records of your husband's previous stay in hospital and I'm afraid that the lung damage that he suffered then has not helped him. When we last spoke, you mentioned your son—have you told him anything about your husband's situation?'

'Oh, yes. My son is working in Bristol and I've spoken to

him on the telephone, but I told him to stay where he was. He could accomplish nothing by coming back.'

'Well, you may feel you would like him here now. If so, and you care to give Mrs Parsons the details, she will telephone him with your message. Now—perhaps we could go to your husband, Mrs Hawke?'

Garbed again in gown and mask, she re-entered the Intensive Care Unit. The array of medical equipment was still present and Joe Hawke appeared not to have moved since she had last seen him, but it was immediately noticeable that his pallor had increased and his breathing sounded shallower.

Colonel Yates pointed to the comfortable chair beside the bed, saying, 'I would like you to talk normally and conversationally because I am hopeful that an atmosphere of normality will start off a rally. Touch can also be important.'

Fiona settled down in the chair, her thoughts in a turmoil. Beneath it all she was feeling grateful that Hilary Grey had telephoned her earlier that afternoon. Hilary had, of course, been through it all—the whole way through—and her quiet, comforting manner had been extremely helpful, and, in retrospect, it still was.

The desk telephone rang. 'Sue? This is Linda. About tonight. I rang up the station and they don't know when the trains are going to start. Here, your operator is an old cow, isn't she? She wasn't going to let me speak to you. "We don't allow private calls, you know." That's what she said.'

'They've got some funny rules here. So what are we going to do this evening?'

'LBC put out a news flash which said that they were dealing with two bombs at Vauxhall. We heard it on my friend's trannie. I don't think they'll get the trains running in time. We might as well have a night out, eh?'

'OK. I haven't had one for a long time. Where shall we meet? What time?'

'Well, I finish at 5.30. Let's meet at the café at quarter to six for a cup of coffee before we go up west. Can you borrow some money, Sue?'

'OK. There's a good film on at the Gaumont. If we can get in, that is. It's going to be very crowded if people can't get home.'

'Yeah. Still we can try. I better ring off now before that operator of yours cuts me off. See you later, Sue.'

'Oh, blow her, she don't worry me. Bye-bye, Linda.'

A great deal warmer, and rested, Andrew Johnston felt that his tiredness had retreated under the influence of the pies and coffee. His concentration on the car problem had not blinded him to the fact that the advancing afternoon and the fog's return were conspiring to deepen the gloom in the tunnel. With Wheelbarrow gone, he no longer had its powerful lighting available, but he needed to use both hands, not have one tied up with holding his own lamp all the time, so the engineers' department had brought up their modern generator-driven mobile lighting set.

Clad once more in his protective gear, he carefully positioned a number of extremely powerful lamps in the tunnel, aiming them at the car. The Consort was now drenched in their concentrated glare and, carrying his tool kit and lamp, he felt as if he were leaving the shadowy wings to advance on to a floodlit stage. This time, there was an additional advantage—the lights were also making the working area appreciably warmer.

Peering through the broken window, he could see the control box lying where the second shot had projected it, at an angle on the floor behind the front passenger seat. The floor and seat were now carpeted with glass granules from the shattered windows but the thing that attracted his attention was the jagged hole at the rear of the seat. The beam from his lamp pointing into the hole showed him that it extended through the metal seat base and the bottom of the car.

There was no way that he was going to lift that boot lid, and he was certainly not going to open any doors by hand, but the one thing that he needed was to see what, if anything, lay under the seat swab. Before he could achieve that, though, he needed to open the nearest door by remote control, and that meant using a line from behind cover. So, with infinite care he put his hand through the broken window, raised the door button, freeing the lock mechanism, and then, delicately but firmly, he attached the end of his nylon line to the door handle. Carefully playing out the line, leading it around one of the buses across the road, which would give him a better angle for the tug, he moved off around the corner, taking up position in Parry Street.

Glancing towards the Range Rover before giving a warning call, he could see the tall figure of another explosives officer, Don Reynolds, newly arrived and talking quietly with Clem Jones and Peter Barwell. The steady, determined pull on the line went on, it seemed, for ever, as the nylon line stretched to its limit before the feeling of release came as the car door swung open. No explosion was heard. Tension relaxed, he waited for a couple of minutes, then joined the group at the Range Rover. The first thing he wanted to know was what Don was doing on the scene. Don told him that having cleared up a letter bomb in a general's Belgravia home, he had been sent here by Bernard Gregory to see if he could help.

Although he had earlier refused the offer of help from Frank Norrie, Andrew's antipathy towards visiting colleagues who arrived unannounced, was at this stage of the day, mellowing. What really made the difference, though, was that of all his colleagues, this was the one he respected most. Don Reynolds' wide experience included an extremely full tour in the early, hectic days in Northern Ireland, and his thoughtful, calm approach to any problem mirrored Andrew's own attitude. The fact that he had obviously come forward on foot, leaving his driver and his vehicle back at Pendennis House, said everything.

Andrew brought him up to date on both devices, and then ran through his proposed action for the car bomb, emphasising his intention to complete the clearance on his own unless further difficulties arose. The bomb under the bridge was a different matter, however. He would welcome a helping hand there, particularly in getting together some equipment and vital information.

Clem Jones broke in on the conversation. 'You haven't forgotten that the dogs are still at Pendennis, have you? The powder wagon has just arrived there as well.'

'Thanks, Clem, but they'll have to wait, won't they? So long as they stay back. I can do without them down here.'

Don Reynolds left to get things organised for the bridge. Back at the car, Andrew Johnston found the door wide open, the nylon line still attached to the handle. He stood and studied the seat swab very carefully. Since he still needed to get a sight of what, if anything, was underneath, it would have to be turned over remotely. He would certainly not try to do it any other way—the job had been going on too long to take silly risks.

Returning to the car later, having successfully repeated the rope-trick and dislodged the swab, he could see that a number of polythene bags had been lashed into position with detonating cord. Even without disturbing them he could count at least twenty bags, every one filled with a deep cream-coloured granular substance. The smell of almonds which had been present ever since he had first looked in through the window was now overpowering—it had to be 'co-op sugar'. This improvised explosive, very sensitive to blows or friction, and with a highly toxic vapour, had first been identified in a bomb in the Co-op supermarket in Belfast. The IRA had used it often until they realised that it produced medical problems, continuing to use it, but on a reduced scale. Given the location of its first discovery, and its appearance, it was inevitable that the Army should have given it the nickname by which it was always known.

The detonating cord, Johnston could see, snaked away

from the explosive to disappear under the seat-back in the direction of the boot. His next move was going to involve getting the back of the seat out of the way so that he could see into the boot. Working very delicately, he undid the clips and at last succeeded in lifting the seat-back out of the way.

It was no surprise to see a further problem staring at him. The detonating cord disappeared into the zipped-up top of a medium-sized tartan grip standing centrally in the boot. An electric detonator was firmly taped to the cord, with a pull switch attached to the boot lid.

Isolation of the detonator and clearance of the charges in the seat and in the tartan grip—one hundred and fifty-five, and sixty pounds, respectively, including the boosters—followed as routine operations. After more than seven hours the railway was now safe. Time: 15.55.

Back at the Range Rover, Andrew found that Don had returned. He had brought his own vehicle up now, and he pointed to the back of it, where Andrew could see a large, blue plastic bucket and a long piece of wood with a pulley fixed at one end.

'You got it then,' Andrew said. 'Good.'

'Yes. And I got a message through to the launch and they've agreed. Everybody is in the picture, and I'll do it from the top. All they need to know is when you are going to start. Warlock's bringing the media gang down now, and the message has gone out to the railway that they can get their lot started again. They reckon it will be another three-quarters of an hour before the first train can leave Waterloo.'

'Thanks, Don. If that circus is on its way down, we'd better sod off out of the way. The sooner they get finished, the sooner we can get started on the bridge. It's getting colder and this fog is getting worse. We won't have a lot of time.'

'That's right. Warlock says he's going to allow them ten minutes and then do his star turn back at Pendennis. I wonder if he'll end up with a job in the BBC as well?'

'Before they get here, ask the Exhibits boys to get the explosive into the powder wagon—they can put the complete seat and the grip in as they are. That'll keep the cameras away from it. Mind you, they'll have to get a bloody move on. If we're not careful, Warlock will be putting his foot on the car and posing for the "Great White Hunter" bit!'

'That'll make a change from putting his foot in it!'

Fifteen

The road block in Nine Elms Lane, to the west of the new Covent Garden market, consisted of two frozen traffic PCs, their BMWs standing across the east-bound carriageway. Bored, frozen stiff, hungry, they had been in position for the best part of two hours. The deepening gloom and worsening cold were not helping either.

Hunched up against the cold, they had just about exhausted every conversational gambit and were reduced to staring gloomily ahead while waiting for relief. Stuck out there they couldn't even indulge in the standard time-passer of playing cards. To the average Trafpol, purgatory consisted of policing a road devoid of traffic while totally cut off from refs (refreshment) and a pack of cards.

The enveloping sound-barrier of their white helmets was penetrated by the sound of a car approaching from the direction of Battersea Dogs' Home, to their astonishment, on the other side of the central kerb.

'The stupid bugger's on the wrong side of the road, Alec!'

'We'll still have to stop him, the crazy git. Doesn't look as if he's going to stop on his own. Hasn't even got his bloody lights on!'

A short obscenity later, Alec's BMW was off its stand, engine running and accelerating after the car, blue lamps flashing. Weaving through a gap in the central kerb, he caught up and waved the car into the side of the road, short of the Wandsworth Road lights.

Leaning the BMW on its side-stand, he dismounted; as he walked deliberately back towards the car, its driver's window slid down and a woollen-hatted head appeared. The gaudy colours of the hat and the black face spoke volumes—this was unlikely to be a calm discourse!

'What's the matter, man? What's all the fuss about? You going to be harassing me, man?'

'Will you get out of the car, please, sir? I would like to ask you some questions.'

'Why's that, man? I can hear you from here!'

'Please turn off the ignition and get out of the car, sir. We can talk better that way.' Reaching forward, the constable grasped the door handle, pressed the button and opened the door wide. A flurry of running footsteps behind him announced the breathless arrival of his superintendent.

'What the hell's going on here? Who is this madman? Doesn't he know what's going on here? Get out of that car! And, how did he get past you, anyway?'

'Look man, don't talk to me like that. What's coming down here? Isn't your man coming down heavy enough for you? You harassing me, man! I know my rights!'

'Perhaps I can explain, sir. This man drove past us, without lights, and on the wrong side of the road. We didn't have a chance to stop him—the fog's getting thicker and with no lights he was through before we knew.'

'Right then. Nick him and get him out of here. Leave the car. The Explosives Officer is just about to start again on the bridge and this area has got to be kept clear.'

'What's this about an explosives officer? What you nicking me for? You only doing this because I'm black! You pigs is all the same, harassing us because we's black!'

A few minutes later, after a virtuoso solo performance from the superintendent, embracing both the constable and the car driver, the latter was out of the car, as the saying goes, well nicked and moving sweetly. One more hazard dealt with.

Standing at the granite block at the beginning of the bridge, with helmets and clothing on, Andrew and Don looked over towards Millbank. Andrew pointed out the counter box still in position on the pavement with the cutter lying beside it, and explained the position of the main charge and the access to it that the ladder gave him. Upstream they could see the launch, which was holding off near the river bank, about two hundred yards away.

Under the combined influences of the advancing afternoon and the deepening fog, the area was growing appreciably darker, so much so that the glow from the street lamps was now more pronounced. With the cold intensifying, Johnston felt that they should get on with the clearance as soon as possible, so he flashed a call-forward in the direction of Don's waiting Range Rover.

When the vehicle drew near them, Don's driver off-loaded the bucket, the timber and an extra supply of rope. He had also brought a radio. As he was preparing to leave, Andrew asked him to pass a message to Bert Smith to say that it was proposed to start operations promptly at 16.30 and that he was equipped with radio now. Messages like that were best passed face-to-face. It dealt with the problem of eavesdroppers.

Calling up the launch, which had also been equipped with a local radio of its own, he checked the system and then, accompanied by Don Reynolds, moved forward to the ladder. It was the work of seconds to disarm the counter box so that it could be moved carefully out of the way, together with the cutter. They lashed the length of timber firmly into position on the railings above the concealed charge and, having fed a rope through the pulley, attached the bucket to it, fixing a second rope to the bottom of the bucket so that it could be tilted from above.

Moving back to the granite block, Don Reynolds called up the launch with a request to start operations and then returned to the ladder where Andrew had already put on the safety line.

The launch came nearer to the bridge, with an extremely powerful searchlight, specially shipped in the last half-hour, focused firmly on the black plastic bag jammed in the girders. Taking up station on a line parallel with the bank and about one hundred yards from the bridge, the coxswain, by skilful use of the powerful engines, concentrated on keeping the launch stationary.

A selection of tools loaded into his jacket pockets, and carrying his lamp, Andrew Johnston climbed over the railings and took up position on the ladder, level with the explosive. Down in the water, Andrew could see a small dinghy edging slowly towards the plastic bucket now hanging motionless near the surface of the water, and he watched and helped with hand signals as the crew of the launch manoeuvred the dinghy into the right position. Scrambling from the ladder on to the girders next to the explosive charge, he studied it carefully. To his surprise, it was actually contained in three separate back plastic bags packed close together like chestnuts inside their prickly case.

With his Stanley knife, he made a short, careful horizontal cut in the uppermost black bag. The cut, about four inches long, sagged open like an idiot's mouth to reveal a second layer of black plastic. The smell of almonds became stronger. Cutting delicately through the second layer he uncovered a white plastic bag similar to those recovered from the car, confirming his nose's identification of the improvised explosive.

After two further cuts he was able to insert his hand into the bundle, and, feeling tentatively around the white bag, he started to ease it forward from its resting place. With his attention wholly concentrated on that bag, he drew it slowly and warily clear to deposit it thankfully into the bucket. Angling the beam from his lamp into the now empty space, he could make out a length of detonating cord encircling the next bag. Nothing else unusual was to be seen.

The first hint of cramp—as yet nothing more than a localised tensing of the lower calf muscle of his left leg—now insinuated itself into his concentration, and he decided that it would be a good idea to get back up to the pavement where he could relax and put Don in the picture. As he was, rather stiffly, changing position, the swinging lamp beam passed across the rear of the charge and a slightly sagging thin shadow caught his eye.

It took a fraction of a second for this fleeting image to register on his brain. He swung the beam back and this time saw it plainly—a length of twelve-pound-strength, dark brown cuttyhunk fishing line, anchored to a nearby girder and leading into the back of the black bag. In the dismally poor lighting under the bridge it was a miracle that he had seen it.

The need to relieve the cramp was becoming more pressing. Stretching out his hand, he caught hold of the ladder and nearly toppled into the river. Fog, now beginning to freeze, had deposited a fine film of treacherous ice on the wooden surface. Slowly he started upwards, the growing fatigue hanging heavily around him like a weighted cloak.

When he joined Don Reynolds, now back at the granite block, both ropes in his hands, Andrew Johnston immersed himself, almost sensuously, in relieving exercises.

'Don, can you get in touch with the launch and find out if they're having any difficulty? They're doing a bloody fine job but it must be a bit of a strain keeping the dinghy in place. I've seen the stuff down there now and it's obviously co-op in three-pound bags, with the whole lot in three black dustbin bags, double thickness. However, there's an interesting optional extra—a pull switch at the back of the charge to stop us dragging out the whole lot in one piece. Bloody well hidden, and I was lucky to see it! Is there any more coffee about, do you think?'

'The coxswain says he can cope for some time yet, so there's nothing to worry about there. Andy, you're looking bloody knackered and frozen—how about me giving you a spell? I reckon you can do with one! Anyway, how much longer do you think it'll take? You've been at it all day and there must be quite a bit left to do?'

‘I’ll be OK, Don. Thanks all the same. I’d like to clear that switch myself first and then we can see how it goes. I’ll tell you what I could do with, though—a pole about eight feet long with a nail or a hook in its side at one end. If they find that they can’t keep the dinghy in position there’s no way that we can move the bucket towards it at the present.’

‘Fair enough. My driver can bring that when he brings the coffee. But, Andy, don’t go on too long—we’re too near the end to take chances. Don’t forget that most of our chaps who got the chop in Ulster were either too tired or took one risk too many.’

‘OK, OK. You’re getting to sound like my dearly beloved. I reckon we’ve got about another three-quarters of an hour to go. I’ll do the next stint and then come up again.’

‘See that you do. You know what you’re like when you get involved in something.’

The door bell’s single, shrill call filled the Clissold Park flat, arousing Brendan O’Loughlin from his reverie with a start. He relaxed when he heard the coded follow-up. In the heavy silence that followed, he moved to the doorway where he responded as arranged by rattling the Yale knob, to be answered by a quietly spoken identification from outside. Admitting the two men standing at the top of the stairs, he closed the door quickly behind them.

Having got their heads down as soon as they had reached their Drayton Park hide-away, Padrig Coyle and Tom Walsh knew nothing of Sean McAllister’s unerring progress from one disaster to another. A radio newscast concerning the end of an IRA hostage situation, coming during their meal, had produced a distinct lowering of confidence. No name had been given but, for both of them, the instinctive reaction was to think of the Glaswegian. If he had talked before he died . . . The tension grew during their journey to the pre-arranged meeting at the Clissold Park venue.

As he entered the flat, Coyle blurted out, ‘Did you hear the news, Bren? About the hostage, the shooting in Islington? Do you know who it was?' Noticing the unexpected silence in the flat, he went on, 'Where's Sean? Was it him?'

'The three o'clock news only said that a hostage situation had been resolved. It didn't say who was involved.'

'Ah, but there was a news flash just before we came out! It said that a man had been shot dead and he was thought to be an IRA gunman. Was it Sean?'

'I don't know,' O'Loughlin replied. 'The last I saw of him he was headed for Paddington.'

'Why did you split up?' Tom Walsh asked.

'He dropped a full magazine on the pavement in Edgware Road this morning and then threatened everybody with his automatic. The man was such a bundle of nerves there was no knowing what he would do. The only thing was to leave him to it. He's become a definite liability, a danger.'

'You're right, Bren,' Walsh said. 'You couldn't do anything else—them's the rules. No sense in reinforcing failure. Anyway if it is him, and he's dead, the danger's gone.'

Coyle had been thinking. 'If it *was* him, do you think he had anything on him to connect him with us or this place? Maybe we ought to be moving now, before they get here.'

O'Loughlin looked at him sharply. He was almost certain he could detect a note of incipient hysteria in Coyle's voice. He needed to deal with it quickly. 'No,' he said firmly. 'If we leave in a panic there'll be mistakes made. We've got to get more information before I decide what to do.'

Now in the sitting room, the three of them sat down, after O'Loughlin had inserted a coin into the meter and lighted the gas fire. The air was crackling with tension. The strident call of the front-door bell froze all three into immobility. From one of them the uncontrollable, pervading smell was that of fear. The pressure of events was taking its toll of Padrig Coyle's small remaining stock of resilience. The coded addition to the first ringing of the door bell allowed them all to breathe a sigh of relief.

Brendan O'Loughlin recognised the slight figure, clad

anonymously in blue jeans and anorak, and invited her in at once. Geraldine Donnelly was the courier.

'I didn't know whether you would still be here,' she said.

O'Loughlin looked up from unzipping the grip. 'Why shouldn't we be here?'

'Because of the news, of course!' Coyle shouted. 'That bloody idiot McAllister taking hostages! Christ, you don't seem to realise he may have given the lot of us away.'

'Calm down, Padrig,' said O'Loughlin. 'And for God's sake leave off the shouting. You want all the neighbours to hear?' He exchanged glances with Walsh. Coyle was clearly on the verge of breakdown, and they would have to watch him carefully. 'In any case, we don't know for certain that it was Sean.'

'We do,' Geraldine Donnelly broke in. 'There was a news flash on LBC. It said the siege was over because the man had been shot dead, and that he had been identified as Sean McAllister, the gunman wanted in connection with the murder in Warren Street this morning.'

'The murder? The bloody idiot! The bloody fool! We're done for!' Coyle's voice rose hysterically again.

'Shut up!' O'Loughlin spat the words at him, simultaneously slapping his face with such force that Coyle was sent sprawling to the ground.

'What else did it say?' Tom Walsh asked the girl.

'Nothing more about Sean. It said two bombs had been found at Vauxhall and were being defused.'

'Let's hope the bastards miss one of the wires. What have you brought us, Geraldine?'

Although Padrig Coyle was huddled in a corner of the room, snivelling to himself, the atmosphere became a little less tense as Brendan O'Loughlin examined the contents of the grip. There were timing mechanisms, electric detonators, pull switches and batteries. Not many of each, but enough to replenish the ones that had been used in the last few weeks. This ASU had placed several bombs in London, and stocks were low.

Checking completed, Geraldine Donnelly left straight away. She was an important link in the organisation, extremely vulnerable, travelling alone, and it was necessary to limit her exposure as much as possible.

Crouched once again between the girders, Andrew Johnston had discarded his helmet. He had found it restricting and distracting earlier, and space was very tight under there, to say nothing of the fact that with the visor down he would be sweating too much. Its absence, however, made quite a difference to his working conditions—for a start his head was very much colder and, far more important, the surrounding noises came flooding in more aggressively, demanding attention and seeking to distract him from his task. Water noises from the river, traffic noises, the transmitted echo through the bridge structure of some under-employed buffoon kicking the metal railing to restore some degree of circulation to his steadily freezing feet—all of these would have passed unnoticed in the enclosed world created by his helmet with its ear-enveloping rubber pads.

Stretching precariously over the bitterly cold water flowing some ten feet below, he was reaching out to cut the dark brown line when his right foot slipped on the gelid metal support, destroying his precarious balance and pitching him further under the bridge. For an instant, the unthinking instinct of self-preservation took over, blinding him to the consequences, blacking out his normal analytical thought processes and guiding his actions be sheer instinct.

Desperately avoiding any contact with the black bags, he succeeded in grabbing a diagonal metal strap, part of the bridge's strengthening tracery, and clung on in a muscle-cracking posture, fighting frantically to overcome gravity and regain control.

Looking back on the incident later, he could not remember whether, in those terrifying seconds, he had actually closed his eyes or if the optic nerves had cut off the picture signals to his brain, but when his sight was restored he became aware that the bridge of his nose was firmly pressed against the cord, taking up all the slack.

The booby-trap was now poised to destroy him, and the bridge, to negate all the painstaking moves that he had been taking over the past few hours, all his concentration and effort, years of training and experience cancelled out by a crowd of terrorists and a slippery foothold.

Sixteen

The 'PM' news announcer on Radio 4 had completed the headlines. *Parts of London are still at a standstill after a day of unprecedented terrorist activity. In the early hours of the morning an explosion in Greenwich seriously wounded a civilian explosives officer who is now critically ill . . . Liverpool Street station was closed for . . . Road traffic is still at a standstill at Vauxhall Cross but the railway service into and out of Waterloo station is due to recommence at five o'clock. A massive car bomb there has been safely defused and a second bomb is being dealt with . . . The area of Shaftesbury Avenue is also closed. A suspect bomb in a doorway is being dealt with . . . During the day other incidents have been dealt with at Holborn and Oxford Street . . . At Warren Street near Tottenham Court Road a gunman shot and killed a bank messenger. In what is believed to be a connected incident, a woman and her two children were taken hostage by a man who was later shot dead by a police marksman. The man, who claimed to be Sean McAllister, a member of the Provisional IRA . . . A statement by the Home Secretary is due to be made in the House of Commons this evening . . . The Metropolitan Police says that traffic in London is not likely to return to normal until tomorrow morning and . . .*

Brendan O'Loughlin switched off the radio and silence descended—an uncomfortable silence made noisy by the thoughts of the three men.

Padrig Coyle was calmer now, but he was the first to speak.

'I hope the English bastard dies! The bomb man at Greenwich—I hope he bloody well dies!'

'It makes no difference whether he dies or not,' O'Loughlin said. 'Dead or badly wounded, he's one of them, and because of that the Mets are going to be buzzing around like flies on a midden. Now's the time for caution. No unnecessary movement. No pubs. We'd best stay here and keep quiet.

'Yeah.' Coyle paused, and then added softly, 'I'm all right now, Bren. Sorry about earlier—it just got to me, that stupid bastard Sean.'

'Sure,' said O'Loughlin.

Tom Walsh was full of outrage at the time and energy wasted. Placing the bomb under the bridge had taken a lot of strenuous effort with nerves screwed up tight, getting tighter all the time. 'They've been bloody quick at Vauxhall! How have they done it?'

'This is London—they work differently here. In Derry they'd all be sitting around looking at it yet. Besides, one or other of them, or both, may still go up. Even if they don't, we'll have caused the biggest disruption ever, and that's worth something.'

'What, stopping a few people using the trains? That's nothing, Bren, and you know it.'

'Sure, Tom. But we can't win 'em all. Wait till next time.'

'When's that going to be?'

'I don't know. We'll be told. Meanwhile we've got to sit tight here for a few days. One good thing—it's nearly two and a half hours since Sean was killed—we can't be certain, but I reckon that if they'd got anything out of him about this address, they'd have been here by now. As long as we keep quiet, we should be all right. The boys will tell us if there's any pressure building up in the area.'

'Pity we haven't got a TV,' remarked Walsh.

'We have,' O'Loughlin told him. 'In the other room. Only black-and-white, but it works. We can watch the news later. There's sure to be a spokesman on, giving away more than he's hiding. In the meantime, what about a game of cards?'

After the game had been in progress for some time, O'Loughlin, struck by a sudden thought, asked, 'What about the garage, Tom? Is it secure? There's some co-op still in there.'

'Oh, there's nothing to worry about, Bren. I made bloody certain it was properly locked after the car was taken out. It looks all right from the outside. Just like the others.'

Andrew Johnston's life did not flash before his eyes—perhaps that only happened if you were drowning, he thought wryly. He was simply aware of a feeling of sheer bloody rage against the futility of his situation and the realisation that if he did not do something quickly he was going to lose—to lose in a totally undignified and unprofessional, yes, unprofessional, manner.

He could feel the strength leaving his arm and the straining left leg. Reaching behind himself with his right hand—the knife had already disappeared into the river below—he groped around and, finding another metal strap, clung to it with a vice-like grip. Pausing to seat his left foot firmly and regain control over his breathing, he drew himself steadily backwards, letting the cord slacken once more.

Crouched again in his original position, reaction set in—his heart thumping and legs trembling, the coldness of his head accentuated by the layers of sweat now breaking out. Speaking impulsively to himself, he said, 'What a bloody awful job! I shan't forget Vauxhall in a hurry! A drunk, a dog, some bloody fool in a clapped-out dinghy, a poxy chopper, and now this! I'm either a bloody tired man or I'm getting old. Don was right—the sooner he takes over, the better.'

Selecting a pair of wire-cutters from the tools in his pockets, he stretched out again, concentrating fully on securing good foot and hand holds, and cut the brown line about six inches from the charge.

He eased another bag of explosive out, still taking care not to disturb the detonating cord. Two more bags followed into the bucket before he signalled Don to lower it to the dinghy, where a pull on the second rope tipped out the bags. A fine degree of judgement was required for this, since dropping them from too great a height, even on to wood, could risk setting off that particular explosive.

With much of the detonating cord now exposed inside the black bag, he could just make out the end of an aluminium detonator poking out between two of the small bags. Gently separating them, he could see that the detonator was taped very firmly to the cord, with a PP3 battery nestling beside it. One detonator wire, sheathed in yellow plastic insulation, led to the battery's snap connector which he carefully prised off before withdrawing the battery and dropping it safely into his pocket.

Ten more three-pound bags, in two loads, were fed into the bucket and tipped into the dinghy in a joint effort that was beginning to work even more smoothly with practice. The pile in the dinghy was growing, and there was already more than forty pounds there, all snatched from its menacing position under the bridge.

A quick cut of the tape separated the detonator from the detonating cord, and Andrew slid the now empty black bag delicately away, exposing the pull switch in its position on top of the middle bag.

The sound of the breaking window sped along the dark, foggy, back lane like a gunshot, to be followed almost immediately by the tinkling sound of glass landing on the concrete floor inside the garage. Young Jimmy Atkins, with the detailed knowledge of the terrain born of years of mischief, raced down the narrow side alley leading from the lane as if all the demons in Highbury Fields, screeching and squawking, were in full pursuit.

His instinctive reaction had been to run, and it was succeeded by blind heart-stopping panic as his flight was arrested in mid-stride by the grip of a heavy hand shooting out of the darkness to grab his jacket shoulder.

‘Not so fast, you young villain! Who are you and where do you think you’re going? Ah! It’s Jimmy Atkins! I’ve been waiting to catch one of you young buggers for a long while. There’s been too much trouble from you young tear-aways around here lately.’

Ma Scroggs was a frightening prospect at any time—short, fat, indeterminately over fifty, garbed in one of a succession of floral cotton pinafores, she was the eyes and ears of the neighbourhood. For all of her tank-like bulk, when provoked she could move with the speed of a striking cobra.

To twelve-year-old Jimmy she was the avenging angel made flesh, and he had urine running freely down his leg to prove it! Just then, the Dickensian tableau was thrown into sharp relief by the headlights of a cruising Panda car which came to a halt at the mouth of the alley. Winding down the window on his side, PC Fred Robson enquired, in his best talking-to-the-public manner, into the circumstances surrounding this mystery. Then he got out and went towards the garage.

Shining his torch through the hole in the shattered window, he saw that the garage was empty. As he turned away he became aware of a faint odour, familiar to him because of a previous posting to the Bomb Squad. He switched on his personal radio and put out a call for the duty officer, and then returned to question Ma Scroggs and her small captive.

Ten minutes later, the duty officer was listening, rather impatiently, as PC Robson continued, ‘There’s a particular IRA explosive that smells strongly of almonds, and that’s the smell that’s coming from inside. The garage is empty, but Ma says that there’s been a car in there for a couple of days. Two colours but she doesn’t know what type. Jimmy Atkins, the kid, says it was some sort of Ford and that he’s seen two men going in and out—one blond and one with black hair. They kept the doors closed all the time, and a third man came to visit—a well-built chap who didn’t stay for long.’

‘Well, it’s all a bit iffy but I’d better see if I can smell it too. Almonds, you say, Fred?’

‘Yes, guv. It’s not very strong but I’m certain of it. I smelled a bag of it once in the lab at Woolwich, and you don't forget that sort of thing.'

Meanwhile, Ma's better nature had come to the fore, and Jimmy was munching a biscuit in her untidy kitchen, his nether regions wrapped in a towel. Noticing his little 'accident', her ire had disappeared in a twinkling, and, despite his vehement protests, she had bustled him into the kitchen and stripped off his jeans and pants.

Bowing to the massively outraged dignity of a twelve-year-old, she filled a chipped enamel bowl with hot water, handed him a face flannel and Lifebouy soap, and left him to wash himself while she rinsed out his garments and hung them on the fire-guard to dry in front of the kitchen range.

Back on the bridge once more, Andrew discussed progress with Don Reynolds while sipping a most welcome beaker of piping hot oxtail soup that Clem had brought forward for him. The black plastic bag lay at his feet, with the detonator, pull switch and battery placed on top, awaiting the opportunity to pack them properly.

'Don, there's more than forty pounds in that dinghy now and I think the rest will be straightforward. I should watch that ladder though—it's getting to be slippery and it's pretty dodgy when you climb on to the girders. There's not a lot of room under there and that water looks bloody freezing.'

'Thanks. Two black bags, did you say?'

'Yes, one on top of the other, both about the same size. I couldn't see any complications. The detonating cord is still there, of course, so there must be a booster somewhere.'

Twenty minutes later the back of the job was broken. Don Reynolds had successfully gutted the second bag, finding the booster charge—five pounds of gelignite. The total haul was forty-three three-pound bags of explosive, plus the gelignite—that would have caused a hell of a lot of damage—and shaken the wax out of a number of ears! All of it was now being towed in the dinghy to Nine Elms Pier, to await disposal.

Both Range Rovers now appeared, and Bert Smith and Peter Barwell crossed the pavement with outstretched hands, intent on congratulations. Andrew Johnston formally handed back the scene to Bert, then set about organising the work of clearing up. Time: 17.25.

Seventeen

The detective-constable finished making the proper record of the incoming telephone call, entered the time of receipt as 17.32, and turned to the Bomb Squad duty officer standing beside him. 'There's an interesting message from the station officer at Highbury Vale, guv. It could be the garage—at least that's what Fred Robson reckons.'

The duty officer took the message from him and read it very intently. He did not show emotion—there had been quite a lot of apparently promising messages in the past which, after days of hard, tiring slog, had produced a final zero. All experienced detectives had learned to live with that, particularly at this early stage of the investigation, but it didn't make it any more entertaining.

'Fred Robson—he left just after I came here—what's the SP on him? Can we rely on him? This could be a pretty good break if it's true.'

'He was good value when he was here. He's a memory man and worked on a lot of good jobs. Doesn't get excited over much, like some we've had around here. He's due for his stripes pretty soon. He's been selected.'

'OK. Pass it to the action squad straight away and I'll go and see the Guv'nor. If it's that good he'll want to know now.'

Some ten minutes later he returned to say, 'A team's going up there straight away—if it's any good the sooner it's followed up the better. I think one of the explosives officers should be there as well. If there's anything in it he'll have some work to do, and it will save hanging about. Give them a call and lay it on will you?'

'They may have a problem finding one straight away. They're pretty well committed at the moment, guv.'

'That's their problem!'

'Detective-Sergeant Brockway here . . . I'll do my best to get one there but we've been pretty busy all day you know . . . I know all that, but we're bloody thin on the ground. I'll ring you back.'

Pressing the cradle switch to clear the line, he dialled the number at Pendennis, asked to speak to Bernard Gregory, and when he made contact gave the Chief Superintendent all the details and asked if Don Reynolds was available. Within minutes Don's evening was organised and he was on his way to a meet at Highbury Vale—scenes like that had a high risk potential and needed to be dealt with by professionals, real professionals. The booby trap potential was high and a well-meaning, half-informed enthusiast blundering about created danger rather than reduced it.

Bernard Gregory was just starting to enquire about the general picture when a constable came into the room to tell him that the Minister was arriving accompanied by the ACC.

The procession reached Vauxhall Cross looking decidedly chilled, their transfer from warm offices to the freezing, foggy world having been rather violent, even allowing for the heated cars that had been used in its achievement. Junior ministers and senior officers did not normally have direct access to, or need, bad weather clothing.

Finishing off the scene record and listing the exhibits, prior to moving off to Nine Elms Pier, Andrew Johnston eyed the approaching cavalcade with tired, cynical amusement. He had seen the performance popularly known as 'visiting stations' too often to be greatly impressed.

The junior minister, Sir Adrian Noxon (Con. Forest of Dean) was in the van, flanked by the ACC, Joshua Goodbody, and Pat Warlock—in at the kill and running true to form. The remainder, Macleod and Gregory among them, followed roughly in columns of threes in a variety of garbs and steps. The media, outflanked, had disappeared, unbriefed, towards deadlines, the press conference, or selected watering holes.

'Minister, this is, er, Major Johnston, the Explosives Officer who has dealt with these two devices—he has, I am informed, been heavily engaged all day.' Apart from not having been provided with a decent brief, the ACC found difficulty in unbending, his gifts not extending to fluent conversation outside his limited professional circle. He took refuge in the well-worn subterfuge of giving the man on the scene a chance. 'It would perhaps be best, Minister, if he were to explain the situation here himself.'

Under the brooding gaze of Pat Warlock, piqued and poised to wrest back the initiative from a member of the civil staff, Andrew drew a comprehensive picture of the day's happenings. Without drama, without extravagant language or lyric turns of phrase, in the strictly flat, didactic style of a military appreciation, he led the Minister through the story, paying particular tribute to the actions of the launch's crew and the part played by Don Reynolds, now on his way to Highbury Vale. Nor did he forget the explosives sniffer dogs whose exhaustive confirmatory search of the area had only recently been completed.

It was now that Sir Adrian became the victim of his political training and experience and wandered into an unexpected, if minor, minefield. By asking Andrew his opinion about terrorists, he thought that he was merely making polite conversation with a worthy but inferior being—one of the chores that a member has to undertake in his progress through life.

'Speaking as one who has been actively engaged in fighting them for a long time, Sir Adrian, I must confess that I hate their guts! And I most strongly support bringing back the death penalty!'

A momentary dumbfounded silence greeted this remark. No one was supposed to voice an opinion of that sort in public, and particularly not to a politician whose adherence to the anti-hanging lobby was possibly the best-known thing about him. The ACC barely managed to stifle a strangulated sound of disbelief, and certain other members of the gathering could be seen having difficulty in keeping straight faces.

Sir Adrian, his missionary enthusiasm now aroused, was quite willing to continue the discussion. 'But surely, Major, it's been accepted that the death penalty is not a deterrent. It only makes martyrs of them.'

'Well, Sir Adrian, it may not be a deterrent but it certainly stops them doing it again. There ought to be more to punishment than compulsory TV and a choice of menus. Chaps who do this job would feel a lot happier if there was an element of retribution. They also reckon that nobody in authority wants to understand their opinion.'

It was time, Sir Adrian decided, to abandon the engagement. 'Thank you, Major, it's been a most interesting talk.'

Urbane to the last, the Minister asked a few more questions, congratulated Andrew Johnston on his efforts and, under the guidance of a self-satisfied Pat Warlock, made a lightning tour of Vauxhall Cross and the bridge, before speeding back to the protection of the Palace of Westminster, cocooned in the enclosed, heated atmosphere of the ministerial limousine.

In the practised, professional hands of the police and the railway staff, river, rail and road traffic shivered its way back towards something approaching normality in the fog-bound darkness.

Shaftesbury Avenue, in the heart of London's West End, could be a policeman's nightmare. The first quarter of a mile of this once fashionable thoroughfare curved gently but garishly from Piccadilly Circus to Cambridge Circus through the multi-racial ragbag known as Soho. In an area liberally besprinkled with theatres and cinemas, the Avenue was normally packed with the heavy volume of traffic using a main through-route.

The early evening bustle of the area was completely overshadowed by the tense calm which gripped the Avenue between white-taped barriers at Rupert Street and Charing Cross Road, and which was centred on Wheelbarrow swaying its caterpillar way along the road surface through the freezing fog past the lurid glass, chrome, and plastic shop fronts in the direction of Cambridge Circus.

Controlled by Frank Norrie from the darkened interior of the Transit parked outside St Anne's Church in Dean Street, Wheelbarrow's target was a trendy, glass-fronted boutique on the Avenue's northern pavement. Sometime earlier, a plastic carrier bag had made its unauthorised appearance, concealed behind a rack of regimentally suspended dresses, frilled and flounced with the Paisley-patterned modernity of the twenties, tent-like expressions of the individuality of youth in an Aladdin's cave of over-priced, swinging fashion.

A disbelieving assistant's examination of the carrier and its contents, her languid approach transformed in a flash to bowel-loosening activity, had set in motion the train of events bringing Wheelbarrow to the road outside.

Left thumb back, right thumb forward, operating the joy sticks, Frank Norrie spun Wheelbarrow to the left, pointing it towards the boutique's open door. Then both thumbs went forward to compel it to stumble up the kerb, across the pavement, through the glass tunnel and into the entrance. Weaving its way hesitantly through the hanging racks, Wheelbarrow came, eventually, face to face with the carrier bag, standing quiescent and totally devoid of visual menace, near the right-hand window.

Nosing delicately into the top of the carrier, Wheelbarrow sent back an illuminated picture of yellow wires connecting a loaded battery holder to a partly tape-obscured pocket watch and the aluminium detonator almost wholly inserted into a large plastic-covered bundle. Decided on his next operation, Frank Norrie pressed the control to withdraw Wheelbarrow's boom, accidentally knocking the watch in the process.

Chattering animatedly, like a pair of jays, oblivious of their surroundings and insulated by adolescence against the cold, Linda and Sue talked their way up Macclesfield Street towards Shaftesbury Avenue. Without even noticing, they had stepped over a length of grubby white tape lying across the pavement with one end tied to a convenient cast-iron railing. The police dilemma of insufficient manpower had shown its face once again. With every access point to cover, with the need to keep people away from windows, to re-route traffic, answer questions and attend to a hundred and one problems, Macclesfield Street was fleetingly unmanned.

As the boom struck the watch, time caught up with the boutique. Set on the minute hand, the watch had been timed to detonate the bomb nearly three hours earlier, but a poor contact had left it hanging, poised to function without warning. Watching the monitor screen, Frank Norrie saw the picture spin crazily in the instant before, with a blinding flash of white light, it went blank. Fifteen pounds of violent high explosive under the impetus of its detonator erupted with a fury not experienced in Soho since the war.

The thunderous roar of the rapidly expanding gases tearing themselves triumphantly free from their chemical prison reverberated through Soho, the sound even penetrating New Scotland Yard's double glazing a mile away. A dense cloud of evil black smoke ballooned out of the boutique, overtaken by lethal missiles in the form of glass shards and lengths of metal frames.

Linda, slightly ahead of Sue, had scarcely left the shelter of Macclesfield Street when the blast wave tossed her sideways, screaming hysterically, to lie on the ground, bleeding profusely from a number of glass-inflicted wounds, and shivering with shock. Sue, unscathed in the last protective shadow of a building, stood, white-faced and shaking from head to toe, before adding her overwrought, uncontrolled sobbing to the rising chorus.

The form that their evening out was to take had now been ordained. In no way was it going to be classified as entertainment. Unforgettable, yes, but enjoyable, no.

Wheelbarrow lay, severely damaged, on its side, slammed against the boutique's side wall, one track missing, almost hidden under a tattered pile of erstwhile fashion, mute and broken. The four-hundred-pound explosives officer's stand-in had done its job.

Amidst the rising clamour of a multiplicity of two-tones and bells, a chief superintendent muttered, 'Jesus Christ! If that's a controlled explosion, I don't want to hear a real one! It's going to take all day tomorrow to sort out this little lot.'

Joshua Goodbody sat stiffly at the centre of the long veneer-topped table standing on its dais, with Commander Warlock on one side and Commander Macleod with the head of Press Bureau, on the other.

The Metropolitan Police was in communication with its paymaster—the public. At the end of a very long day of unrelieved success it was now engaged in doing its best to bolster the political standing of yet another Home Secretary, of yet another in a long series of governments that had declined to grasp the nettle of terrorism by the neck. Bonhomie within limitations in the best traditions of selectivity was the simple pre-ordained style.

The battery of upwards-pointing cameras—a well-established technique to improve the image of those being photographed—interspersed with local defence microphones, was locked in on the hostages in an atmosphere of cynicism unsullied by tobacco smoke. With the exception of a few scattered guerrillas, everybody present on both sides understood the rules of low-key contests applicable to the present skirmish. Bland innocence, feeding fast balls to the slips and uni-directional oral sensitivity were all held in operational reserve.

At half past six the conference began. The hymn was still on Macleod's brain. *Thou art very weary*. But there was also hope—*Night shall end in day*. The head of Press Bureau took a deep breath and started to speak. 'Ladies and gentlemen, may I welcome you to this conference, which it is hoped will help you to understand the build-up of today's activities. But first, Mr Goodbody, the Assistant Commissioner (Crime), wishes to offer his apology for the delayed start. This was not done to be awkward but was imposed by the pressure of events.'

He took the assembly through the events of the day, starting with the tragedy at Greenwich, the disruption at Liverpool Street, the shooting and the hostage incident, the extended operations at Vauxhall and the successful clearance of two letter bombs and a number of hoaxes and innocuous items. An account of the Shaftesbury Avenue bomb came last, and shocked them all. When they began to ask their questions, he told them that a full report was not available and that all he could say was that, as far as was known, there had been no loss of life, and although the boutique was almost totally destroyed, the damage did not appear to extend greatly beyond it, and the essential services in the area seemed to be unharmed.

He began to fill in various background details, and then, in a moment of silence, he dropped a pebble in the pool—the mention of the Minister's visit to Vauxhall. The ripples spread, and he could sense their indignation.

Inevitably it was Dwight Hoffman who put it into words. He turned angrily to Macleod. 'How come we weren't told about this? Godammit, it must have happened at least an hour ago.'

'We have done our best to keep you advised,' Macleod said, a little stiffly. 'It just hasn't been possible to . . .'

Nicotine starvation added to alcohol deprivation had not sweetened the Kansas Bear's personality. 'This is press censorship. You may be sure, Commander, that my readers back in the States will hear about it, and they won't like it one godammed little bit.'

Seeing Macleod somewhat at a loss in the face of this unprecedented attack, Warlock stepped smoothly in. 'Ladies and gentlemen, I'm afraid that we did not know of the intended visit until after most of you had left Vauxhall. The

Minister had only a limited amount of time available due to pressure of business in the House.'

'Well it sure looks like a set-up to me!'

Pat Warlock had learned a long time ago that when dealing with a hostile questioner the way out was often an abrupt change of subject to something else of prime interest. Ignoring Hoffman, he said, 'I am sure you will all want to know whether there is any official view on who has been responsible for today's incidents. It looks as if more than one group has been active and, with the telephone threats, the background could be Irish, but there is a lot more work to do before we can be certain.'

'Mr Warlock! Can you say whether you've had any success with your enquiries today?'

'Well, as you know, I've spent most of the day at Vauxhall at the area of greatest threat, but I can tell you that members of my team have been very busy throughout London, making enquiries and seeking information. It appears that there has been some success, but I am unable to comment any further, I'm afraid.'

This let loose a flood of questions from different parts of the room. Now that Pat Warlock had taken over the conference there was much more chance of getting usable answers.

The direction of the questioning switched unexpectedly with an intervention from Brian Morton, the television reporter. 'Could we have a better statement on the incident at Islington? The Commander said that a man was shot by a police marksman. Does this indicate a change of policy?'

Before Warlock could answer, Joshua Goodbody intervened. 'Mr Morton, isn't it? Yes, I have remained silent so far, preferring to leave the conduct of this conference in the hands of my officers who have themselves been involved in today's operations. Now, however, you have posed a question which I feel it is incumbent upon me to answer.'

'Pompous old fart,' one of the reporters muttered.

The ACC turned in his direction. 'Did you say something?'

'No—just clearing my throat.'

Goodbody allowed the hint of a smile to play briefly about his lips. 'Extraordinary how critical a clearing of the throat can sometimes sound.' The reporters laughed. 'Now, Mr Morton, you will agree, I think, that there were quite exceptional circumstances at the siege in Islington. A woman and two children were being held hostage by an extremely disturbed gunman. The latter opened fire on the husband and gave every indication of wanting to kill him. And if he had succeeded in that intention, there was every possibility that the mother and two children would be similarly treated. The policeman had no alternative but to shoot.'

'Mr Goodbody, you say that there were unusual circumstances. Surely every hostage situation is unusual? Or are we now accepting certain hostage scenes as being usual? But what I am really concerned with—are we moving towards a shoot-first policy?'

'No, Mr Morton. Every incident must be dealt with on its merits and our aim will always be to resolve such situations peacefully as far as is humanly possible.'

Seizing his opportunity, Pat Warlock deftly brought the proceedings to a close at this point, blandly turning aside further attempts to keep the pot boiling.

Fred Robson, standing in the fog by the row of four garages, was glad to see Don Reynolds and the others. The freezing cold was beginning to bite into him and, in any case, most of them were old friends. The exchange of greetings over, he launched into a monologue about the circumstances that had led up to the request for their attendance. Preaching to the converted, he had no difficulty in convincing them of the possibilities in the situation.

With the Range Rover positioned so that its headlamps and 'bat lamps' lit up the garage, Don Reynolds began his examination. Standing on his tool box and using his mirror through the broken pane, he carried out a detailed survey of the inside surfaces of the doors. Nothing significant could be seen but, shifting his scrutiny to the general interior, he could see a shiny black plastic bag lying in one of the corners, partly concealed behind a five-gallon oil drum. He could also make out that a large pane of glass in the rear window appeared to have been replaced by a sheet of hardboard, cut to size.

Twenty minutes later, he was in through the rear window, and the doors, checked and cleared, were wide open. The black bag had yielded sixty-seven pounds of explosive but, apart from a supply of clear plastic bags (three-pound size), nothing else of interest had turned up.

Eighteen

Back now in the explosives office, Andrew Johnston glanced at the clock set high up on the wall. Eight p.m.—exhibits all dealt with and initial paperwork completed (full reports and statements would come later). In contrast to the dark, freezing, foggy outside world, the office was a calm, well-lit, warm haven whose soporific atmosphere was making its mark.

Tension dispelled, fatigue was now creeping over him, sweeping forward in a languorous tide, and he was grateful for the cup of fortified Marine's tea that Clem Jones had placed on the desk in front of him. Reaching for his telephone he dialled home. Jean answered and he spoke. 'Hello, dear. It's been a long day but I'm finishing up now. Everything's OK. No bits missing! We'll be leaving shortly. After I've had a shower. Have you cooked anything?'

'No. I didn't know what time you'd be finished. When you have one of these days it's a waste of time trying to plan anything.'

'Fair enough! Clem and I will stop on the way for a good spaghetti. We won't be late.'

'They said there's been another explosion this evening. In Soho.'

'Yes. Frank Norrie had a bit of bad luck, I gather. But nobody badly hurt. Anyway, there'll be some gear for Oxfam. It was a boutique. How's the old girl this evening?'

'Oh, she's all right. We've been over the same old stories for the umpteenth time. I know them all by heart now. Hilary phoned this afternoon. She still follows what's going on quite closely. Have you heard any more about Joe Hawke?'

'Not lately. As far as I know he had a pretty bad spell earlier on and Fiona is staying down there. The last I heard he was holding his own but it doesn't sound too good. Well, my dear, I'll sign off now—I'm pretty hungry. See you later.'

'All right. Don't be late. Don't forget you're on early again in the morning.'

Don Reynolds was still engaged at Highbury Vale and Frank Norrie was at the rear of the Guildhall where a late call had dragged him away from contemplation of the Shaftesbury Avenue extravaganza.

Trains and buses were back to normal as if nothing had ever happened, except in the West End where the police were going quietly potty trying to sort things out.

Nicos Georgiou was with his wife Ethel, to whom he had given a somewhat fictitious account of the day's adventures. Usually she refused to join his arguments, but at the moment the two of them were engaged in a dispute about the possible purchase of a new inflatable, and she was keeping her end of it going in a way which Nicos found highly satisfying. Perhaps it was her way of showing that she was glad he was back safe and sound. The two boys were upstairs asleep.

Washington Leroy, drugged eyes unfocused, was in good hands awaiting an operation.

Mrs Mary Higgins, widow of the late Sid Higgins, sedated, was the cynosure of a group of friends in Rayleigh trying desperately, yet knowing the certainty of failure, to push back the threshold of heartbreak.

Fiona Hawke, her son's arm awkwardly encircling her motionless shoulders, sat weeping quietly in the Colonel's office.

Following a tip-off, the police searched a flat in Battersea. There they found—left behind in an evidently hasty departure—certain interesting items apparently connected with the Greenwich incident. The flat's occupants had disappeared.

Three other Irishmen, playing cards, were unaware that their garage had been raided. And only a few policemen knew that in Sean McAllister's pocket had been a scrap of paper with a scrawled address.